Please return this book on or before the due date stamped below

1

s
is
n
r
d

8532
ion of

Bruce Fellows

That Quiet Earth

I lingered round them, under that benign sky; watched the moths fluttering among the heath and harebells, listened to the soft wind breathing through the grass, and wondered how anyone could ever imagine unquiet slumbers for the sleepers in that quiet earth.

Emily Bronte, *Wuthering Heights*

Matador
9 Priory Business Park
Kibworth Beauchamp
Leicestershire LE8 0RX, UK
Tel: (+44) 116 279 2299
Fax: (+44) 116 279 2277
Email: books@troubador.co.uk
Web: www.troubador.co.uk/matador

ISBN 978 1780881 324

British Library Cataloguing in Publication Data.
A catalogue record for this book is available from the British Library.

Typeset in 11pt Minion Pro by Troubador Publishing Ltd, Leicester, UK
Printed and bound in Great Britain by TJ International Ltd, Padstow, Cornwall

Matador is an imprint of Troubador Publishing Ltd

This book is for
SUE BRIERLEY

One

The great lime at the end of the garden is beginning to shed its leaves. They swoop and pirouette in the breeze like carefree souls until they end their brief careers in stillness on the grass. They fill me with a strange foreboding. On the table at my side is a three-line item from *The Times*. It stopped me short the other day and hurled me back, as vividly as if it were yesterday, to the clear sky over France on that evening in November 1918 when I led the day's final patrol.

The sky was a blue parasol above. The earth from so high was slightly curved at the horizon. England was a low smudge faintly visible far away west. A deafening roar from the engine filled my head. A leather helmet gave little protection against it. Obeying Mitch's precepts and using the only sense useful to me in the icy cold of eighteen thousand feet, I constantly scanned the sky in front and below, but especially behind and above. I was seeking the enemy I was supposed to kill but particularly searching for those who might want to kill me. I was conscious above all of my responsibility towards the men who followed me that no enemy should surprise us.

Just behind me, twenty yards away on either side, rising and falling as if on a gentle invisible swell were two olive drab SE5s identical to mine. Their pilots, Zin Zan and Telfer, togged up like me in fur helmet, goggles and face mask, also quartered the sky. From time to time their wings would rock and glint sunshine at me from taut canvas surfaces.

Then to the east, a thousand feet below and perhaps three miles distant, I picked out dots against the sky. I rocked my wings and turned away, raising the nose to climb. Three minutes later and a thousand feet higher, I slowly edged back towards the dots. The sun was safely behind us as the dots slowly became aeroplanes and their top wing extensions became obvious. A group of six Fokker DVIIs was flying two thousand feet below. I checked obsessively behind and all around, cocked both guns, and prepared for my stomach to rise into my chest and the pain to start in my ears as I put the nose down.

The dive would have taken thirty or forty seconds. Our speed reached a hundred and sixty perhaps. That was time enough to see the dark shapes beneath us grow, take colour and become swaying, bobbing, almost living things hanging nearly motionless in relation to us, as they flew seventeen thousand feet above the grey-green patchwork far below.

I chose the leader. His tailplane was painted dragonfly blue. The straight black crosses on the upper wings were outlined in white on the pink, purple and green of the camouflage the Germans habitually used. I put my face to the Aldis sight and watched him fill it. I fired Vickers and Lewis guns together. Their chatter rose above the engine's roar. I smelt the cordite and saw my tracers converge on the fuselage and spray around the cockpit. The machine below me at once turned to the right. I thought I'd missed and the pilot was warned but instantly the machine turned again and then again and was spinning, making a spiral of the smoke that was pouring from the engine. The pilot was wounded or dead, and the spin was involuntary or a hopeless attempt to escape despite having a smoking engine three miles up.

I dived on down, screaming from the pain in my ears but also from bestial triumph. I was too fast to turn and we'd tracked the Huns till almost the end of our patrol. As I pulled out, I looked behind and saw only the other SEs following. Two trails of smoke had formed behind us, marking against the celestial blue the killings that we fled homewards from.

For some reason it was that fight of many that the article in *The Times* brought to my mind. Perhaps because that was when I fulfilled my ambition to dive on a Fokker and send it down, as we had wanted to, Billy and I, and as he already had. I read the article over and over.

> *The Victoria Cross won in September 1918 by 2ndLieut. William Love RAF, has been sold in auction at Sotheby's for a record £65,000 by Love's elderly niece.*

"Love's elderly niece" could only be Pippa, a six year old elf when I first saw her.

The article occupied my thoughts all through that day and so clouded my sleep that I dreamt that night that Jessica returned to me. Her face had the look it had that ravishing day that Billy and I passed through the archway, luscious with the scent of honeysuckle, and crossed the lawn towards her in the sun. At his call, she started up from the rose she was kneeling at and, turning, bathed us in her sudden joyful smile.

I woke at once, damp with anxious sweat, and got out of bed. At ninety-seven, that has become a very slow and precarious business. I went to the cane chair by the window and sat with a blanket around me, watching the sun appear and banish shadows from the garden. I spent those first hours of the day composing a letter for the small girl to whom, if youth had the wisdom of old age, I would perhaps have been stepfather. It was a letter full of memories and some regret, which Pippa answered on the telephone.

"How wonderful that you should write," she shouted, we are both a little deaf, and how wonderful that we should still both be alive, she might have added. "Mother passed on twenty years ago." I hadn't really feared a centenarian's reproaches and I felt a pang that I had missed Constance.

"For years," Pippa said, "you were like a legend to me, half-remembered, and I used to wonder why your name was mud. Later of course, I came to realise why from things that mother said. I used to see your name at the flicks just before the director's, 'written by

George Bridge', and I'd wonder if it was you. I knew you'd gone to America you see. Then I learnt it *was* you and you grew still more glamorous in my eyes. Was Carole Lombard as lovely in the flesh?"

She was of course but it was at Myrna Loy's house on a St Patrick's Day in the late thirties, after the premiere of *Seven Deadly Sinners*, which I'd written for her, that someone sang 'Danny Boy' and wartime ghosts thronged in. They drew such weeping from me that I was packed off in Miss Loy's limousine to come to later amid empty bottles and the remains of smashed up furniture in my rented apartment. After that I was able to admit to my mind again memories I'd repressed for many years, though all my life I've never learnt to master them.

"I'll send my great-grandson, David," Pippa said. "He won't mind. I sold it for him. To buy a partnership. It's too far for me. I've got a funny hip. How undignified old age is. Dear George. Though I was so young, I remember knowing I was in love with you myself."

David came today with the gift, or rather the loan, that Pippa promised of Billy's diary, soon to join his medal in the RAF Museum. Nudged by that, by the logbook I've never thrown away, and by a journal that I kept in the year after the war, I'm writing this record of my thoughts of now and the events of three generations ago. Despite the years that have passed, and my current frail body and white hair, those events are as clear in my mind as when they happened during those few months when I was nineteen and lived life at a pitch I've never experienced since. Any moment then could have been my last, in that summer and autumn when those ghosts that made me weep at Myrna Loy's were living, breathing companions of mine.

And who am I doing this for? Well, when he entered the lounge of this residential home I live in and swung his eyes around the room for me, David pushed his long fair hair back with a sweep of his hand that was so like Billy's that for an instant I felt my heart stop. So I will leave the disc for David, the great-great-grand-nephew of a hero. He may do with it as he chooses but not, I will insist, until Pippa has made her final journey and joined me in the grave. Pippa has the constitution of a very lady-like ox, so that may be some time.

Really though, of course, it's for myself that I'm grasping this final chance to tell my story, hoping to lay more than my dead comrades' ghosts, hoping to settle thoughts that have lain buried inside me for years but which, now revived, stir me as those curling leaves do from the lime. Don't think though that it's just a tale of war I have to tell. I spent the prime years of my life concocting stories for the masses on the silver screen. I know that all stories are love stories. This is a love story, too.

I remember it still so clearly. It was a bright June day in 1918, and as I stumbled from the train, which had taken us unknown to each other to the station nearest to our new squadron, I almost dropped my valise on Billy's exquisitely polished brown shoes.

"What ho, young Icarus! Mind the shine," he said.

His quick glance of course had spotted the new wings on the breast of my RAF tunic. Then, "Have a gasper," he said and his slender fingers offered a silver case.

His hair was long and straight and on the darker side of fair. His nose was straight too and his upper lip long. When something angered him, I later learnt, his head would tilt back and lip and nose would give him an imperious air. But when he smiled as he was doing now, calling me his "new chum", he revealed large gleaming teeth, perfect apart from one incongruous gold molar on the left. Together with those blue eyes that still had the smile and twinkling animation I later saw them lose, the gold tooth lent him an exciting piratical look. Then the sun came out from behind a cloud and caught his hair and seemed to lighten it from within, surrounding the smile in a blond halo.

I was nineteen, fresh from grammar school and still in the perpetual state of half-terror I'd endured since joining up. To me, as our train pulled away with whooshes of steam and left us on that country station in sudden unattended, blackbird punctuated silence, this jolly, cigarette-cased, golden-haired pirate was mythical, god-like. It was me, I thought, suddenly exhilarated by this meeting, who should have called him young Icarus.

A corporal collected us and our luggage. "Come on, George," Billy said, instantly intimate.

As we drove off out of the station courtyard crammed into the front of the Crossley tender, Billy engaged the corporal in conversation in the natural way I grew to envy.

"How long have you been in the service, corporal?" he shouted above the engine.

"Since before the war, sir," the corporal shouted back, "when the Corps was tiny, sir."

"Like McCudden, eh?" Billy said, naming the hero of most new RAF pilots; a boy in the Royal Engineers, an air mechanic in the Royal Flying Corps, then an observer, soon an officer and now a captain and a top-scoring pilot with a Victoria Cross.

"Ah, yes sir. I knew him then, sir. But he was always a deep one. Always thinking and reading. A great man, sir. And great with an engine."

So they talked, while I gazed at the passing countryside with a town boy's eyes.

It had started with my Uncle Fred.

"Flying's the game, George," he said, trying to guide me away from the trenches. "Those buggers go home to dinner and a bath, while you've got to patrol No Man's Land in the mud or take a ration party three miles up the line in the dark." He was only five years older than me, my mother's baby brother, but when we spoke he was moustached, with wound stripes up his arm, and suddenly seemed a real uncle's age. He was a captain in the West Kents and lucky to be alive I realised a few months later, but like millions, his luck didn't hold.

"And they get their pictures in the paper," he said.

I too had read of Albert Ball, the teenage Hun Killer, and Leefe Robinson, the Zeppelin Strafer and what Fred said confirmed my own delicious longings for glory. So a year later, having persuaded my parents

8

of the comparative safety of the air and having good eyesight and the right reactions and having been taught by the new Smith-Barry dual control system to take an aeroplane up and land it and to do various things with it in between, I sat silent as Billy and the corporal talked on about engines. Until, that is, my attention was caught by a speck in the cloudy sky ahead. It rapidly swelled and grew wings and became a biplane. I nudged Billy and pointed.

A hundred yards away at tree top height, the aircraft banked and crossed the windscreen in front of us, left to right, revealing square wing tips, a blunt nose and square tailplane. Red, white and blue roundels stood out stark against the unbleached linen of the underside of the wings. Then in a trice, the aeroplane reversed bank and, large and daunting, swept towards us and over our heads, swamping our speech and the sound of our engine in a sudden, short, deafening roar. We all three ducked involuntarily and Billy and I gazed through my window as the tail disappeared over the hedge.

"Cracking buses, SE5s, aren't they, George? I'm glad we're not on Camels."

So was I. Camels, single-seaters built by Sopwith, were reported to kill more pilots than the Hun did. If you let go of the controls, it was said, a Camel would immediately rear up and the force of the rotary engine, fixed to the propeller and turning with it at a thousand revs per minute, would send the aeroplane into an instant right hand turn from which a spin would develop.

SE5s had sensible stationary engines, much more solid and much faster. McCudden flew one. Ball was last seen entering a cloud in one. All the big Hun getters flew them and we were going to as well. Ergo, the unspoken thought, as Billy and I grinned at each other, squashed into the cab of the tender, a mile from our first posting, we would become big Hun getters too, on this beautiful, sensible, fast machine.

But first of course, we had to learn to fly them properly.

"How many hours have you got on SEs?" Major Quaife asked us in the squadron office that Billy had led me straight into. On my own, I would have lurked outside for crucial moments, straightening my tie, rehearsing my reporting speech, mentally practising my salute.

"Eight, sir," Billy said.

"Nine, sir," I said.

"God's teeth! It gets no better, does it?" the major cried to the ceiling.

He was twenty-four or five I now suppose but to me then he seemed a different generation. His eyes didn't blink as he gazed at you but there were lines around them that grew deeper when he laughed, though laughter hadn't caused them. The DSO and MC ribbons beneath his wings, of course, commanded an instant respect that he retained even when buried under a pile of bodies in a game of mess rugger.

"Very well," he said, resigned, "we're here for three weeks while we work up. You'll fly twice a day and if you've got any spare time you can go up again."

He stopped as we heard an SE fly past, throttled back for landing, and stared across his desk at us. Then he began one of the many short speeches designed to keep us alive that the experienced in the RAF were always delivering to the inexperienced.

"That machine," he jerked a thumb over his shoulder at the noise, "will keep you safe and sound or kill you. Which it is depends on you. It will only do what you make it do. So find out all the things you can make it do here, while no one's firing machine guns at you."

He creased his eyes up, gazing at us as if searching the sun for German aircraft. Then he suddenly laughed.

"Don't look so glum the pair of you. You're a long time dead. Now then, you're both in 'A' Flight, Captain Mitchell, one of our coloured troops, Canadian. Bloody Canadians seem to run the RAF. Top notch pilot though, he's got twenty Boche, so if he says something, listen to it.

"Dinner's at eight. Slacks are in order. Bar opens at seven. You're not teetotal, are you?" We shook our heads. "Thank God for that. But watch the sauce. You'll be drinking with chaps who've had a year or two in the trenches and some chaps find it amusing to get other chaps tight. Especially when they're not used to it. So learn to handle it. A convivial mess makes for a better squadron spirit, and nothing helps conviviality more than a few drinks. Questions?"

"How many Huns have you got, sir?"

The major was clearly taken aback by Billy's directness but perhaps he recognised the value of his answer to squadron spirit. After a pause and a brief smile, he told him.

"Fifteen at the moment. The corporal will get someone to show you your quarters, then cut along to the mess. You should be in time for tea. Mitch'll be there I expect."

The officers' quarters, hut accommodation for forty, were laid out as per RAF regulations in an acre of land. The men, of whom there were four times as many, had the same area allotted to their quarters. We left a batman making our beds up and laying out our kit and sauntered off to the mess for tea.

In the intervening seventy-odd years, whenever I've heard any of the show songs of that time, from *Chin Chin Chow* or *The Maid of the Mountains*, songs like: 'If you were the only girl in the world' or 'Anytime's kissing time,' I've been swept instantly back to that RAF mess I entered with my new comrade Billy Love still saying:

"Fifteen's bloody good. I wish I had fifteen."

The gramophone was scratching out 'A Bachelor Gay'. The sun was pouring through the far window. A waiter was circulating among decrepit leather armchairs and negotiating outstretched legs to deliver plates of sandwiches and cups of tea. The officers the legs belonged to had been up since dawn to catch the calm flying weather. Now they had energy only to flip idly through the pages of *Punch* or *The Illustrated London News*.

This is how I would choose to remember the squadron; young men thrown together, whose only duty was to learn to master the aeroplanes they'd been given to play with, something the richer of them would have paid money to do in peacetime. When we had flown each day, our tasks were merely to return to earth and let off steam; to horse around, drink mildly and break furniture. Oh what a privilege it was! And what a lark! At least while no one was shooting at us.

Mitchell was gangling and friendly.

"My father's in the City," I told him. That was close enough and not untrue. Certainly those really in the City used the same suburban trains that he used, though never the same carriages, nor the straps he hung from. He travelled crushed in with the other ranks of the poor bloody infantry of finance before he marched bowler-hatted to his till at the Anglo-Colonial bank.

"Good Lord, no," Billy said, "my father's not that clever. He hunts and shoots, of course, in season but otherwise he's a complete parasite. Gerald Roberts does all the work. It's a small place really, near Taunton. It's been harder since the war began though. The chaps are gone, you see. It's difficult to keep our farms manned."

Mitch nodded sympathetically, clearly not as impressed as I was. Did Mitch's father have farms too? Not a farm but farms, or were farms in Canada so huge that one farm there was like several farms in England? Suddenly aware of the gulf between myself and Mitch and Billy, I marvelled, as I often had since joining up and gaining a commission, at the people the war was throwing me in with.

"Study and get on," my father always chanted when he arrived home late, tired and tormented, from the bank. He would snatch *Comic Cuts* from my hands and ask about my homework. "Look after the pennies and the pounds look after themselves," was my mother's constant descant as she laboured alone at home but for a weekly woman on washday. Our terraced house was dominated at the back by a railway embankment, where, every few minutes, trains passed and drowned out kitchen conversations. I've often wondered if my parents thought their efforts had been rewarded now I was in the RAF and consorting with landowners.

Or was I?

"Some place, that sounds," Mitch said. "My pop's always wanted land but hell no, he's still going to that paper everyday."

A press proprietor I thought.

"I don't know how he does it. He has to read everything backwards setting type. It's a knack I guess. Come on. I'll show you the sheds." I thought then that Mitch was bolstered in the presence of his social superior by his captain's rank. But as I discovered when I heard him speak to colonels and generals, he was genuinely and colonially unabashed by his background. Like the other Canadians and the South Africans, Australians and New Zealanders I met in the RAF, Mitch truthfully considered himself anybody's equal.

He led us along a path by a hedge. Flying had stopped for the day. Pigeons cooed somewhere. The sun was lower but still warm. Billy asked about triplanes now we were out of the Mess and could properly talk shop.

"The Hun's washed them out," Mitch said. "Good job too. They put the wind up me. Too damn splitarse. They could turn inside a Camel. You couldn't keep a gun on them if the pilot was any good. They've gone over to Fokker biplanes. Very tricky buses – never dogfight one. Dive and zoom, that's the game but you can always dive away. Nothing dives like an SE. The trouble is you lose height and height's everything in air fighting. It takes a lot of time and a good motor to go up in the air."

He threw a grin at us. "Like going up in the world, I guess."

In the sheds, lights burned. The wooden skeleton of an SE5, victim of a heavy landing perhaps, stood stripped of its fabric with its tail on a trestle. Riggers worked with plumb lines and spirit levels to tighten the wires that held the ash spars and longerons true. It was a two day job when a bus needed re-rigging. We stood at the doors. The smell was the usual exciting mix of engine oil and dope. Billy hit the taut olive drab fabric of an SE's wing with a flicked finger. It boomed like a drum. I stood on the wing, put my head inside the office and stared at the joystick, rudder pedals, instruments and gun butt.

I did that again the next morning, my head buzzing with remembered instructions, my stomach whizzy with excitement. I was strapped in. The propeller was whirring, the engine roared even through helmet flaps, and the whole machine vibrated. A mechanic was draped over the end of the fuselage to keep the tail down until I waved away the chocks, the mechanic slid off, and the SE jumped forward, eager for the air.

Over the elms I soared, seeing them high ahead, then foreshortened, then the ground through their branches. I trimmed to climb and settled down to clear my ears and enjoy the view for a few minutes, picking out landmarks that would help me find the field again: a church with a tower, the railway line, a road, the leaded roof of a large house set in its own grounds. At five thousand feet I turned in a gentle bank, getting the feel of the machine, searching for the airfield in front of me.

Cumulus billowed away to my right. Below me lay an English mosaic of grey-brown earth, emerald meadows, crops of a green that would soon turn gold, and woods that were russet-brown. In fact the earth that day had its customary beauty that never ceased to dazzle me all the years I flew.

Ours was a new squadron. We were working up prior to going to France. There were a good number of experienced pilots and some new boys, like Billy and me. The flight commanders put us through our paces. It was rigorous training and our flying hours built up satisfactorily. Days passed quickly, though nothing we did was easy. Even landing had its own problems. SE5s didn't like the ground. You had to be sure you crossed the hedge at the right height and throttled back at the right moment to let the bus sink of its own volition. If you tried to stretch the glide because you were too low, you'd lose speed and fall with a neck-jerking crash. If you were too high and too fast and forced the machine down, there'd be another neck-jerking crash. The result of either procedure was an embarrassing hopping progression across the field before assembled pilots and mechanics. When the SE was finally three points on the ground, the pilot was effectively blind because of the enormous engine angled up in front of him. The solution was to kick the rudder from side to side and zig-zag towards your destination. Too unruly a kick though would jerk the aeroplane sideways and tilt it so that a wing tip might dig into the ground and swing you right round or turn you over.

I remained anxious over landings but in a day or two Billy had mastered a three point touch down at almost nil flying speed that made his SE seem to stop in its own length. Then we witnessed the major, after stunting over the field to entertain the mechanics, sideslip down from a thousand feet, like a falling leaf, to land in front of the sheds. The next day while pulling up after a pass at the gunnery target, I noticed Billy's SE three or four fields away sideslipping onto a flock of sheep, which dashed in panic towards the hedge. Two days later, he imitated the major's falling leaf landing in front of the sheds.

Those were the days when aeroplanes looked functional, when you could even imagine yourself building one with a saw and some glue and a pair of pliers. They were wood and linen and wire. We called them buses, crates, grids. Their controls were comprehensible. You pulled this or kicked that and wires were attached to what you pulled or kicked. The wires ran between the pieces of wood and underneath the linen and in turn pulled on another part of the machine and moved it. Then your machine would act on the air differently and make the world revolve. Perhaps the earth would appear to your right or vanish entirely so that only sky filled your vision. Another time, the earth might be all you could see and things on its surface might swell and grow until you pulled on something else and a horizon returned in front of you and things were back to normal. The earth could move gently or violently. Your bus could move delicately through the air like a cat picking its way through a dense flower bed or buck like a horse determined to shed its rider. It all depended on the pilot and how he pushed and pulled and kicked.

I didn't push and pull and kick very precisely. In formation, people gave me a wide berth. I found myself constantly playing with the throttle, surging forward, threatening others with my wing tip or falling back, correcting and over-correcting. It was very tiring. Billy's flying was always neat. He was always in position.

Individually, we practised war stunts. Stall turns and half-rolls with dives away to change direction rapidly. As a flight, we followed Mitch in sudden stomach lifting power dives that drove knives into my ears and made me scream at the engine with the pain. My ears would clear when we stabilised our altitude much nearer the ground but those dives left me with crushing headaches that sometimes laid me out on my bed all evening, dinnerless.

Most evenings though, I managed to eat the usual

stodgy meal in the mess and then sit convivially at whist over the three or four drinks that made even the rotund and florid Keble's jokes seem priceless:

"Have you seen Arthur?"

"Arthur who."

"Arthermometer."

"Is there a Walter here."

"A Walter who?"

"A Walterlean against."

When not flying, we studied the Vickers gun. It fired through the propeller, courtesy of an interrupter gear which stopped the gun when the propeller was in the way. If the Vickers jammed in the air, the cure was to tap it in the right place with the hammer we carried. We studied the Lewis gun, which sat on a curved rail above the top wing, and on the ground we practised changing its circular magazine. The first time I did that in the air, I was so nervous at releasing the controls and stretching out of the cockpit against a hundred mile an hour wind to reach the gun that the magazine tumbled from my hands. I watched it disappearing earthwards, hoping it would not kill a cow or some pathetic farmhand.

To relax and for exercise, we played badminton in an empty part of a hangar and, in the mess, ping pong, at which Billy was vicious, smashing successfully from absurd positions and whooping when he scored.

Every day, Mitch would take off with one of the flight. He'd disappear and our task was to prevent him from reaching a position from which he could have shot us down if he'd been a German. Our general lack of success impressed on me at least, the seriousness of what we were doing. When my turn came, I stooged around at six thousand feet and searched the sky in quarters as instructed. I held up a thumb to cover the sun so that I could look closer to it and constantly glanced behind, grateful for the silk scarf around my neck that eased its incessant turning.

Then, as aeroplanes often seemed to, Mitch's appeared without warning beside me and he waved. I would already have been dead of course but today I had another life. As I saw him slip behind me, I kicked left rudder and skidded sideways. German bullets would have made holes in my starboard wing, now where my head had been. The horizon tilted and the nose fell. I went with the bus and rolled it onto its back until the earth was above me then I dived and heard the engine screaming as I pulled out five hundred feet lower but going the other way. I glanced back and saw Mitch's SE past my tailplane. I repeated the procedure the other way but still Mitch's propeller whirled behind and the ground was closer. I quickly realised that nothing I could do would allow me to escape. Skidding from side to side frantically, I dredged up a piece of advice Mitch had given one day after landing. I put the machine into a vertical bank, earth to my right, sky to my left, throttled back slightly and pulled the stick towards me, glancing back all the time to where Mitch was imitating me.

"If you're caught," Mitch had said, "and you can't dive away, turn and keep turning. No one can hit you like that and all the Huns queuing up to shoot you will get in each other's way."

Bereft of ideas, I kept turning. The turn forced me

deep into my seat and my arms and head felt twice their normal weight. Behind me, Mitch turned, too. I saw a stretch of road below me slowly move away as the wind carried our turning aeroplanes east. What with the spiralling earth and the constant neck stretching to look back that forced my head against the pressure of the turn, I soon felt queasy but just an inclination of the head to the right was enough for my vomit to clear the cockpit rim. I was very conveniently situated for spewing, which I did a couple of times before Mitch waggled his wings and turned for home. I blew my nose and wiped my mouth clean with a handkerchief I then tossed overboard.

"Christ, you're a bloody awful pilot, George," Mitch said, slapping my back after I'd bounced across the field, "but it'll keep you alive yet. I didn't know what you were going to do. I barely had my sights on you once. If I'd missed you before you saw me, I think you might have got away. Stout effort, George!"

Praise from Mitch, I knew, was worth leaving one's breakfast across half of Gloucestershire for. When I asked him how he did it though; how he'd stayed behind me all the time; his answer seemed so obvious. Nevertheless it was the measure of the man that though he told me how to do the same, in France, in my fights with Huns, I never found I had the time to follow his example. He said, "I watched your control surfaces, so I knew what you'd do before you did it."

Of course we spent more time on the ground than in the air and we had men under us. As new boys, Billy and I drew orderly officer duty more often than others. It meant no drinking and a camp bed to sleep on in the squadron office. It meant inspecting the messes: "Tenshun! Any complaints?" But the men knew the required answer, "No, sir," and I never heard a complaint in all the times I did it. We had to take the parade, when the flag was run up and down, and be generally available twenty-four hours a day when not in the air.

But there was plenty of time for yarning in the sun, stretched out on the grass or sitting on an oil drum as we recovered from those monstrous, awful dives and released the engine vibrations from our limbs. Butcher and Baker were a rich fund of war stories. Butcher had survived six months as an observer on RE8s. These were heavy and slow two-seaters and cold meat, if unescorted, for any Hun scout. Baker had been shot down ground-strafing in a Camel during the March retreat and got a lovely Blighty one – a bullet that had nicked his thigh. Recovered now, he hoped the war would be over before we joined it, a hope that Billy and I just couldn't understand.

They told the story of Caldwell. Lapped by flames from his burning engine, he climbed out onto a wing, reached into the cockpit for the joystick, sideslipped down to keep the flames away and stepped off the wing unhurt as his SE flew into a shell hole. Baker spoke of a Camel pilot in his squadron, who, while making a V sign at the machine gunners who had peppered his wing, had his index finger shot off. They both claimed to have seen artillery shells stop in the air for a brief moment next to their machines at ten thousand feet before the shells started their fall to earth. Butcher told of a pilot reduced to pulp by a propeller when another Camel landed on top of his.

Captivated, Billy and I sat on the grass in the sun and drank it all in. We must have looked like the painting of the boyhood of Raleigh, though how much of what they said was invented even today I have no idea.

"Are they making it up, Butcher and Baker, do you think?" Billy asked me one afternoon strolling back for tea.

"God knows. But they're good stories and all possible."

"Having your finger shot off?"

"Why not? There must be thousands of bullets going up in one's general direction."

"But the chances of hitting your finger are tiny. One in a million."

"Or one in two"

"One in two?"

"Yes. It'll be in this position or another. It'll hit or miss. That's one in two."

"I never thought of it like that."

Then I remembered a curiosity.

"Did you know that if you fired your pistol at the horizon and dropped a bullet from your hand at the same time, both bullets would hit the ground simultaneously?"

"That can't be true."

"Why shouldn't it be? Gravity's pulling them down at the same rate."

"But the bullet from the pistol's going so fast."

"But not upwards. Not counteracting gravity."

"I suppose not." Billy sounded thoughtful. "I find it rather difficult to think about, to be honest. You're most frightfully clever, George. Where on earth do you get it from? You make me feel a real duffer."

That was one of Billy's charms. He made you feel worth something. Whatever you said he appreciated and the appreciation always seemed genuine. He also had a talent for confiding, for making you feel needed and that you could be trusted with his secrets. That was how I came to hear about Jessica, his sweetheart, the daughter of his father's agent. They'd known each other all their lives of course. They'd grown up together. She was a lovely girl, good fun, and rode to hounds with verve. But, "If only Dickie hadn't gone west," Billy would say. "I'll have the title now you see."

Our orders for France came through. Three more days of training, four days of leave and then off. The major ordered a squadron practice. We would climb to our ceiling, twenty thousand feet. We dressed carefully. Even in summer, temperatures up there were Arctic. I put on silk and then woollen underwear; two pairs of thick socks; two sweaters; a tunic; a silk scarf; a long muffler; a fur lined Sidcot suit, stained and smelly from the castor oil shed by the rotary engines of the Avroes we'd trained on; fur lined leather boots. Then we dug our fingers into a tub of whale grease, which we applied to our faces, checking each other to see that no part was exposed. Frost bite was a court martial

24

offence. We wiped our hands on cotton waste and pulled on fur lined flying helmets, whose leather creaked in our fingers. Then we carefully cleaned the lenses of our goggles before sliding on silk under gloves, woollen mittens and fur lined leather gauntlets.

I just managed to pass through the door before waddling in the hot sunshine to my machine. I was perspiring by the time I had climbed up and wriggled down into the cockpit.

We took off singly and spent ten minutes taking up formation. I was on Mitch's right. The red streamer that identified him as flight leader trailed out six feet from his rudder. His bus rose and fell gently in relation to mine and the sun glinted occasionally from his goggles as he swung his head from side to side to check his followers were in position.

We climbed steadily east for fifteen minutes, noses above the horizon, then turned and climbed west for another fifteen. The six machines of 'C' Flight were behind and slightly above us, those of 'B' Flight in front and slightly below. I grew progressively colder. My fingers gradually lost all feeling, despite banging them on the padded cockpit rim. I was glad there would be no need to fire guns with them today. We reached eighteen thousand feet, nineteen thousand feet.

At twenty thousand feet we levelled off. One or two of the SEs whose engines weren't up to it hung tails down from their propellers, a little lower than the others. My cockpit was much too tight a fit to wriggle around in to get the blood circulating but the cold could not destroy the breathtaking beauty around us.

Far away west, giant bulges of cumulus, brilliant white against deep blue, were cruising in from the Atlantic like galleons under full sail. Below lay Bristol, tiny from our height, and the Bristol Channel, the Welsh coastline and the River Severn, as if drawn on a map. The horizon had a slight curve.

We'd been up for an hour and a quarter when the major rocked his wings, the signal that the show was over and the flights could separate. I followed Mitch's lead and dipped my nose below the horizon. We followed the coast south-west, descending all the time, but slowly and painlessly. Over Clevedon Pier we circled and turned northeast again. From Portishead we followed the Avon to Bristol. A thousand feet below and ahead of us the Gorge began to rise around the river.

Suddenly, Billy dived under our formation and zoomed up on Mitch's left. He waved his arm and pointed down. I saw Mitch nod his head. Billy put his nose down and disappeared like a stone until I saw the shadow of his aeroplane on the river and managed to pick out just ahead of it the upper wing with its red, white and blue roundels. Mitch turned to us and waved and pointed down. Then he was gone too and it was my turn to rush headlong at the river, fingers and toes now tingling and stinging with returned warmth.

I eased out as trees began to grow in front of me. I throttled back to a hundred and ten and found myself fifty feet above the water, my engine snarling. Rocks and vegetation flashed past. They seemed close enough to touch but in fact were at least two wingspans away on either side. I pulled up a little as I felt the machine buffeted up and down and sideways by wind. I looked down and just spotted upturned faces and waving arms on the deck of a coaster before I flew through its smoke. Ahead of me I caught a reassuring glimpse of Mitch's bus. It had miles of space around it but the grey stone of the cliff side dwarfed it. Then he disappeared behind trees round a bend in this roofless tunnel we were careering down. I banked to follow. A locomotive on the railway line to my right was a dark blur trailing smoke in the corner of my eye. Then the Suspension Bridge appeared; an enormous, terrifying obstacle over my windscreen and gun sight.

Mitch seemed to go lower. Too late to zoom over the bridge, I dipped lower too and at once was through with the river opening out ahead. I climbed to lose speed and floated up over a basin where two steamers lay. To the right, three square redbrick warehouses stood glowering across the river at Georgian terraces stepped up the hillside, genteel and pale in the sunshine.

Billy and Mitch were cavorting over the town, rolling and looping. Even in those days before air traffic control, this sort of thing would cause angry phone calls. But we would be gone tomorrow. I joined them, stunting for the joy of being young and exhilarated and warm again in the sun. Then, attracted by the streets I had strolled along of a Sunday, I throttled back to just above stalling speed and slowly flew the length of what I knew was Royal York Crescent, trying to see through shining windows and waving to startled nursemaids pushing baby carriages along the terrace in the sun.

Mitch waggled his wings and a glance at the clock showed there was just enough time and therefore fuel to flee across Bristol for home and lunch. Buildings and trees appeared and seemed to pass in an instant; you were always so much more aware of speed low down than in the heights. We were a disorganised gaggle now and with the clouds having reached the sun, we threw no shadows on the fields as we sped towards the Church tower that always signalled our return.

Just ahead and above me to my right, was the heavy and rotund Keble, whose cockpit was probably an even tighter fit than mine. Three fields from the aerodrome at two hundred feet, his propeller stopped. The nose of his SE went down and he looked into the office, doubtless switching to the gravity tank. Nothing happened. As I came level with him he glanced at me. I pointed down. He shook his head.

I drew in front and banked around him. On the airfield ahead, one SE had already landed. Keble flew slower. It was clear that the nose of his machine was too high. He was trying to stretch his glide to reach the field, as had been drummed into us we never should. I drew level again, having circled him, and saw the SE's nose come up as it lost flying speed and stalled. The remedy for stalling was to dive but Keble had no height for that. At that moment the machine lost its grace and became an assemblage of wood and metal too heavy to stay in the air. It could only carry Keble down to his doom. The weight of the engine pulled the nose down and over my right shoulder as I circled I saw Keble's bus strike the ground in a grassy meadow. With no sound that I could hear above my engine, the SE crumpled up. I saw the wings fold like a butterfly's over where he sat.

The major gathered us all together still dressed in our flying gear.

"I want you all to remember this well. Keble killed himself. He forgot basic flying skills. If he'd lived, I'd have court-martialled him. Now! I want all of you up again this afternoon and dinner this evening is officially a binge."

They brought his body back in an ambulance. It was broken and twisted, Billy said and the face was mashed and bloody from collision with the cockpit rim and windscreen.

"It's my fault George," he said as we mooched lugubriously around the wreck before dinner. "If I hadn't led that chase up the Gorge, he'd still be here."

"Nonsense," I said. "Mitch was in charge. He was leading, even if you went first. But anyway Keble's gravity tank didn't work. And he shouldn't have tried to reach the field. You heard the major."

After dinner and the usual toasts, the major threw his cap in the air as our ball and a game of mess rugger began.

When I staggered outside for air some time later, I found Billy staring at the stars, glass in hand.

"Poor old Keble," he said. "He was an amusing beggar, wasn't he? 'Is there a Walter here?'"

"A Walter who?" I said.

Two

With the innocent callousness of youth, I'd written to my parents that I'd only have time for a brief visit before going to France. We'd be flying our machines there but before that I was invited to stay with Billy, in the West Country, which I didn't tell them. A letter in my mother's beautiful copperplate with a City postmark came by return. What a pity it was but she understood how busy they kept us in the service. I dashed to London and with a feeling of guilt caught sight of her through our kitchen window as my train passed along the embankment just before I got off at our local station. When I left the next morning my mother pressed a ten shilling note into my hand as she kissed me goodbye. I was to get myself a treat with it. I knew the ten bob had come from her meagre housekeeping savings and since I had eight shillings a day as a second lieutenant and seven and six a day flying pay, I felt worse than if she'd berated me. My father relieved my feelings a little with a farewell I found horrifying. "Keep your chin up my boy and kill plenty of Boche."

I was officially parted with though and could leave for my appointment with Billy. He'd drawn orderly officer and had endured an extra night at the field but when we met up at the station, he was in high spirits. These were smothered when we realised a colonel had already occupied the carriage we selected. Since we'd woken him as we opened the door, it was too late to withdraw.

We lit cigarettes and sat circumspectly as the train rocked us past sunlit hedgerows and river banks. The colonel was thin, wore slacks and was greying, although he was probably no more than thirty-five. There was a tired look to his eyes. He had a black moustache clipped short.

"Flying Corps," he said after a while in a tone half-accusatory.

"Royal Air Force, sir," Billy corrected him.

"Formed on April Fool's Day then, weren't you?"

We chuckled at a senior officer's quip. It was true that 1st April 1918 was the day the Royal Flying Corps and the Royal Naval Air Service, both six years old, had officially merged to form a new independent service.

'What I'd like to know," the colonel leant back and folded his arms across his MC ribbon, "is where the Royal Air Force is," he spoke the words as if they were some kind of affliction, "when there's a push going on. All tucked up because it's raining, I suppose."

I withered and wished myself elsewhere but Billy leant forward.

"Oh, no sir," he said, all sincerity. "You couldn't be more wrong. We're up there, sir, but your chaps have quite rightly got their heads down and don't see us. The stories we could tell you, sir; some of the chaps in our squadron who've been out before! Really stout fellows, sir! I hope we can do a tenth of what they've done when we get out, eh, George?"

"Oh yes," I said, "absolutely."

"One of our chaps was shot down in March, wasn't he, George? Bullet through the leg. Machine-gunned from the ground while he was shooting up front-line trenches. Jerry was lined up ready to go and he knocked a whole trench-full down before they got him. His bus was riddled, had to come down in a field and the wing collapsed as he landed, all the rigging wires shot through."

Billy was embroidering Butcher's tale but he was defending the service.

"And actually," he went on, "perhaps the best work is done further back, sir. If we shoot up a column of trucks, Jerry can't even get to the trenches and has to walk everything up."

"We have our losses too, sir," I chipped in. "Butcher, that's the chap Lt. Love here was talking about, his Camel squadron lost five chaps one day out of eighteen. That's everyone gone west in four days at that rate, sir."

"We still don't see you," the colonel said, not quite placated, "just gnats buzzing around miles in the air."

"Well, sir. The idea is to protect our balloons and two-seaters that are artillery spotting and photographing Hunland. And then, of course, we have to stop Fritz doing the same over *our* lines."

This onslaught seemed at last to have won the colonel over. He offered a packet of Players and finally expressed the fatal curiosity that sooner or later all non-fliers succumbed to, "What's it like in the air, then?" he said.

Billy glanced at me.

"It's wonderful sir," I said. "The jolliest game there is."

"Oh, yes, sir," Billy said. "You must try it some day."

"Too long in the tooth."

"Nobody's too old, sir. Our CO's twenty-five."

The colonel laughed for the first time.

Eventually we descended at one of those long gone restful English country stations with window boxes and a vegetable patch. I can still hear the weary clip clop of hooves as we drove the three miles from it while Billy eagerly questioned the crumbling retainer sent to collect us. Knowing none of the people, I couldn't follow his answers but gazed instead at the country Billy had grown up in. Fields were full but hedges looked unkempt and horses old and weak. The best were taken for the army. The men in the fields were old or weren't men but boys and women, proving Billy's complaint to Mitch about the war.

I sat in shirtsleeves and braces and swayed with the trap as its delicate springing absorbed the shocks of the uneven road. I spread my arms along the padded leather back support, raised my face towards the midday sun and thought that this was a way of life I could get used to. At the same time I wondered nervously whether Billy's father would be very forbidding and how much I should tip the maid.

It was watercress soup for lunch I remember, something I'd never had before, and afterwards an omelette flavoured with chives and fennel, served with bread so freshly baked and warm that butter melted on it. Billy's father was out but would return that evening.

"I'm so pleased that Billy has a good friend in the squadron, George," Billy's mother said as our meal approached its end. "And I'm sure your mother is too. We mothers worry so much in these times you know. It's nice to meet one's boy's comrades. May I give you some raspberries?"

Billy's niece, Pippa, watched me and the raspberry bowl warily from across the table. I teased her in our recent telephone conversation with her anxiety as a six year old, as she was then, that I would eat them all. Of course, she didn't remember.

After lunch, Billy showed me around the grounds. Mown paths crisscrossed through swaying knee-high grass full of clover, vetch and moon daisies. In this beautiful war time dereliction the peacocks' cries grew more mournful even than they had been through lunch. At my bidding we followed the sound, passing between rhododendrons that still bore brown shrivelled remains of flowers, till we reached the ha-ha.

Before us was a large, gently-sloping paddock and far away a hedge, then more fields, hedges and eventually the sea.

"Cracking landing field, eh, George? When the

war's over and Avroes are going for a song, I'll buy one and keep it here and take everyone up and fly around to check the estate."

"You could herd the cows with it," I said.

A peacock cried from back towards the house.

"We've missed it," Billy said. "Come on." I was staring through the rhododendrons, past the pergolas and the red and white roses they bore, back towards the three-storey house, which was originally Elizabethan but much added to later. I heard a noise and turned back. Billy was standing below me in the field beyond the ha-ha. I jumped down to join him.

"Where are we going?" I asked.

"Jessica's."

I stopped.

As suggested by his mother over lunch, he was taking me to his first meeting after months with Jessica, whom he wrote to twice a week. I protested but he refused to go without me.

I crossed the paddock at his side, feeling uncomfortable and preparing to slip away at the first opportunity. I was nervous. I had no sisters or girl cousins. There had been no girls at my grammar school of course, and the RAF had only a few women, so I usually did feel nervous when about to meet a girl. As we passed through the arch of honeysuckle though and Jessica turned from her roses and stood and smiled as she has in my thoughts ever since, and did in my dream the other night, my nervousness subsided. She wore a white blouse and riding breeches. A wide-brimmed straw hat with a red ribbon shaded her face.

They didn't embrace but stood a yard apart holding hands as they gazed into each other's eyes. The all consuming joy in the smile I saw Jessica bestow on Billy filled me with deep envy.

"Mr Bridge," she said, remembering her manners or perhaps wishing to get her duty done, "Billy's written so much about you." She pulled off the straw hat. "I'm so pleased to meet you."

Her hand was warm and its pressure light but it conveyed a feeling of great capability. Her hair was dark and pulled back behind her head. Her nose was slightly curved, her upper lip thin when she smiled and revealed her cheekbones. She was pretty rather than beautiful, which I think helped dispel my nervousness.

"Please call me Jessica. And please come and have some tea with us," she said.

Her naturalness gave me an unusual fluency.

"You and Billy have so much to talk about. I really only walked him over. I'll have tea the next time if I may. I'll go and find a peacock. We couldn't before. And please call me George."

After resisting her protests, I watched them leave. Her left arm was through his. Her dark head, with her hair shining in the sun, was just above his shoulder. The straw hat hung from her right hand, its crimson ribbons flapping by her calf. They turned the corner of a yew hedge and were gone, leaving me alone on the lawn. I went back under the honeysuckle and retraced our steps along the path in the shade of three oaks that I later grew to know so well. Ancient acorn shells crunched underfoot. I swung the kissing gate and squeezed through then crossed the paddock in the sun again.

I remember wandering along the paths between the areas of tall grass, vainly seeking the peacock, whose cry broke through the hot afternoon hum of flies and bees. As I went, I hugged to myself the memory of Jessica's dark brown eyes gazing into mine when she said, "Billy's written so much about you," and revised my previous opinion, knowing then that it was the rapt attention in her eyes that had driven away my nervousness.

Eventually, I abandoned my search and passed through open French windows into the welcoming cool of an empty sitting room. I stared for some minutes at *The Times* but must have dozed off. I woke to find Pippa tapping my leg and wanting me to read a book to her.

I began at the beginning but soon made a mistake, "Once upon a time there were four little rabbits, and their names were – Flopsy, Mopsy, Cottontail and Peter. They lived with mother in a sandbank."

"It's 'their mother'," Pippa said, "'they lived with their mother in a sandbank'."

She knew the story by heart. Then she pointed, "Look! 'Their mother'."

I asked if she could read and she looked up with a very serious face and nodded her confession.

"But if you tell anyone," she said "they'll make me read to myself all the time. Please continue."

I continued, missing no words.

"You're a good reader," Pippa said when I'd read

'The End'. "But not as good as Uncle Billy. Where is Uncle Billy?"

"He's gone to see Jessica."

She made a face.

"Don't you like her?" I blurted out.

"I like her but she's really only a servant," Pippa said. "Her daddy works for Grandpy."

Jessica was invited for dinner and arrived promptly. She looked stunning in a simple grey dress. I was in my uniform since I'd brought no evening clothes, indeed I owned no evening clothes until I went to Hollywood. Billy wore his uniform too though and made me feel more comfortable. I was introduced to the sandy-haired Sir Richard, who was gruff initially but then Pippa, who was allowed up for the pre-dinner gathering, rescued me with an invitation to solitaire. My reading and my gallantry over the lunchtime raspberries had made a friend of me it seemed. Now I was able to demonstrate the system taught me by my Uncle Fred, which always cleared the board of marbles. Pippa was excited and called her mother across to see. Constance was tall, slim and dark with a calm, melancholy smile. Naturally I had also endeared myself to her and was required to take her in to dinner.

I've often dined sumptuously since then; there were many lavishly spread tables in Beverly Hills, but that dinner still seems to me a glamorous affair. The evening sun through the windows warmed the dining room and flashed off the silver and the decades of polish on the oak table and set ablaze the diamonds that Constance and Lady Love wore. Billy looked more legendary than ever with his heavy fair locks falling either side of his face. As I sat surrounded by these fabulous personages, looked down on by portraits in strange ancestral garb, I listened carefully to Constance on my right, and made sure of my silverware by never being the first to start any course.

I enquired about the portraits and heard stories of their deeds at sea, in battle, at court, in bed. Then, since the chief of my ancestors had been a guard on the Great Western Railway, I was pleased to hear the conversation move to Charlie Chaplin.

"He's an anarchist," Sir Richard boomed. "The government should ban his pictures. He's a dirty London guttersnipe, who always thwarts authority."

I listened, too ignorant to reply, and hoped my silence might be taken for wisdom as Billy disagreed with his father.

"He's just a clown," he said. "The men all love him. They work all hours you know, then go to town and see Charlie and come back laughing. He boosts morale. I'm sure Haig would say he's worth a division or something."

Over dessert, candles were lit. Jessica's face turned golden in the soft glow that fell over everything. Then she left, probably uncomfortably, with Constance and Lady Love. At Sir Richard's insistence I had begun to puff tentatively on a cigar when we heard music from the hall and Billy glanced at me, anxious to leave.

The rugs had been rolled away and Constance had

wound the gramophone. Billy glided Jessica effortlessly around on the parquet and I clumsily imitated with Constance, wishing my mother's few front room lessons had been more rigorous.

I was required to continue a sensible conversation while at the same time to move my feet into the right positions at the right speed and press my hand against Constance's waist. Only some minute fractions of an inch of silk separated my hand from the bare flesh whose warmth I could feel through the thin material. Simultaneously, I had to hold her slim hand in mine and not let my eyes drift from her face to my feet, passing as they must, the diamonds at her throat and the soft bosom revealed by her low cut dress. I found the co-ordination required as demanding as flying and very warm work. When Constance said she must slip up to see that Pippa was asleep, I took the chance to step onto the terrace and stroll in the dark, where it was cooler.

I felt an imposter in that house. I despaired of carrying off conversations with members of the family, of playing billiards or casting flies, both of which seemed to be on the agenda. I couldn't ride a horse and had never used a shotgun. Billy, born to it, was adept at all these pastimes. I stood on a terrace by a great urn. Before me, though invisible in the dark, were rose gardens; water gardens; a tennis court, I could at least play tennis a little, and the peacocks which I had still not seen. To my right was a walled garden, whose asparagus I had just eaten, having first surreptitiously watched Billy deal with it. I lit a cigarette and wished I could flee first thing.

A footstep startled me. I turned and saw Constance. The faint light from the dining room candles caught the lustre of the silk shawl that now covered her bare shoulders. She asked for a cigarette. Her face appeared in the flare of the match and she touched my hand as she bent to it.

"Thank you for your kindness to Pippa. With everyone away, or gone, she has so little experience of male relatives. It's very nice to have young men around, if only for a short time. You must come back and stay. When all this is over."

I said I'd love to.

"I'm pleased that you and Billy are flying." Constance said, "It feels more secure somehow than the trenches. I know poor Dicky felt he really had no chance. He was wounded in '15 and killed at the Somme."

"I'm sorry."

"He was quite philosophical about it. He said when one put one's head above ground it would very likely be shot off. When the time came to stand up and attack, he said, one had to do it for the men. One couldn't be afraid, else how could they do their duty. And with so many bullets flying around, only the devil's own luck could keep one safe."

"You're very brave," I said.

"I've wept my tears. Or nearly all. There are only so many one can shed. And after a while one notices the sunshine again. And of course I have Pippa to smile for."

I racked my brain unsuccessfully for some more

41

cheerful subject, not so close to home. I was pleased for the peace of mind of Billy's family that they didn't know about Keble's silly accident and Butcher's five men gone west in a day.

Constance went on.

"It's worse, I think, for Hester. It's particularly awful to survive one's children; to lose one boy and worry for the other. I wish this war would end."

"Amen to that," I said. Yet deep down, young and actually still untouched by it, I thought: but not yet, not till I've dived on a Fokker and sent it down.

While we'd been speaking, a silver sheen had crept over everything, revealing the long grass, rose bushes, trees and hedges that lay before us. The grounds had become an exotic stage set that only needed peopling with a cast in fantastic costumes to bring it to life. I turned to the house. Above the roof a full moon had risen. "How beautiful it is!" I said, glad of a new subject. "It's like… *The Maid of the Mountains*."

"Have you seen it?" Constance cried. "I love the tunes. I do love shows. You shall tell me about it while we stroll in the moonlight." She took my arm and guided me to the steps as if she were eighteen again or as she was perhaps when Dicky was courting her.

We entered that stage set and became players to anyone viewing from a window; a disapproving Lady Love perhaps. Constance put a finger to her lips as we crept past an arbour where two figures, one in a uniform, clung locked to each other on a stone bench. We wandered the mown paths together and turned after a while under the trees where the moonlight was

42

intermittent. Constance showed me the enclosure into which the peacocks were chased each evening to protect them from foxes. One still strutted around and displayed to us, a glorious, breathtaking sight, even in moonlight strained through branches.

Constance had never once released my arm and had even very pleasingly stumbled against me two or three times. As we moved away from the peacocks, I turned my head towards her and found her eyes already on me. She didn't look away but continued to gaze at me. She raised her hand to the back of my neck and pulled my face towards hers until I found myself kissing her. She kissed me back with an ardour that surprised me. We strolled slowly, arm in arm, stopping from time to time.

Later, as I changed for bed, I wondered whether I'd "clicked" as the men would have said or whether for Constance it was merely nice once again to have a young man around, if only for a short time.

The next morning, after a short stroll in the sun wearing a cool cotton suit only a little too large that Billy had lent me, I reached the terrace and made for the open French windows. I sought warm silver dishes, I'd read of them, whose raised lids would reveal kedgeree, devilled kidneys, mushrooms, bacon, scrambled eggs.

I stopped when I heard the 'Gold and Silver Waltz'. In the dining room, Billy and Pippa were dancing carefully around the table. She was stretching up in white muslin and he was bent low in a white open-necked shirt. I watched, anxious not to intrude. When I glanced up, Jessica had approached as silent as sunshine and was gazing as rapt as me into the dining room. She smiled and put a finger to her lips. We heard the last few notes and the final click of the record then saw Billy bow elaborately to his niece and give her his arm to escort her to the breakfast table.

Billy took photographs that day and Jessica later sent them to France for him. He slipped them between the pages of his diary for me to find seventy-five years on. In them, Jessica's hair is up under another straw hat and she wears a pale linen jacket with a buttoned belt and large patch pockets. A full dark skirt that I remember was blue shows three or four inches of ankle. Her neck is open but a white silk scarf hangs around the collar of her jacket. That was her as we went in to join the dancers.

The war perhaps had done for the silver dishes, the sideboard was bare, but Billy rang and soon there was egg and bacon, toast, honey, tea or coffee and we were ready to drive to the sea. Constance, when she appeared on the front steps, seemed much more circumspect in the sunshine that she'd been in the moonlight.

"Do you swim?"

"I love it," I said, watching Billy directing the maid and footman as they took our requirements to the car. Constance looked cool for our trip, twirling a parasol that matched her white frock, which had three bands of large blue polka dots at the bottom of the skirt.

Lady Love, who was not accompanying us, approached me confidentially.

"You will watch Billy, won't you, George? It's the first time he's been alone and he can be so impetuous."

"Alone?" I said.

"In the car. Without Hayter," she replied. The name meant nothing but the tone meant servant.

"Billy's a very good driver," I said, remembering races down the road to Bristol between the Crossley tender and the squadron car, which Billy usually won with a recklessness that had people covering their eyes.

"And of course, he does fly an aeroplane."

"But you're so practical, George."

On my return from the garden the previous evening, I'd impressed Sir Richard and Lady Hester but perhaps also lowered myself in their eyes, by taking a candle and standing on a chair to replace the burnt fuse wire that had plunged the house into darkness. A considerate master and mistress, they hadn't wanted to bother the appropriate servant after he'd retired for the night. That incident had planted a thought in my mind which other observations had fed: the polished shoes that appeared outside my room; the food that arrived at ordained times; the picnic hamper and swimming things now being placed in the car. The rich, in being freed of everyday worries, were in fact enslaved by those who provided their freedom. You couldn't fry yourself an egg in a kitchen ruled by a cook and the mystique of a burnt fuse led you to read casualty lists by candle light. The dereliction of the grounds was further proof.

"It used to look so wonderful," Constance had said in the moonlight as the grass of rampant lawns brushed our knees. "Of course, Hester and I do the roses, but everything else…"

Half a mile down the road from the house, Billy pulled the car up in the shade of a hedgerow oak. I swapped seats with Jessica and got into the back with Constance, who instantly squeezed the hand I let fall on the seat. Whether Lady Love's chaperonage arrangements had been for Jessica's or Billy's benefit, they'd gone west remarkably quickly.

Suddenly, Billy called out that he was thirsty and turned the car from the road onto a track that had us bouncing from rut to pothole and into a yard in front of a cottage. Our noisy arrival there scattered squawking geese and chickens and roused a sleepy sheep dog to have him bark at our door as we pulled up in a cloud of dust.

"Whatever's going on?" I heard a voice call and then a squat figure, wiping hands on a white apron came round the corner of the house.

"Master Billy!" she cried.

"Martha! We're dying of thirst. We've come for a glass of your delicious cider."

Brought from an outhouse, it was refreshingly cool but also sharp. I struggled to finish my glass. Jessica had asked for milk. She sat on a bench with her face to the sun and licked a creamy white moustache from her upper lip.

"I was so sorry to hear about Jem," I heard Billy say.

Three florins shone on the window ledge next to

his empty glass and he'd taken Martha's hands in his.

"It's a great loss."

"Thank you, Master Billy. He was a good lad. But he would join the army. Now we have his name writ in the church and it will have to suffice his poor old mum. Now you come back to us safe, you hear!"

Billy turned the car, scattering geese and chickens again and we bounced slowly away towards the paved road.

"Jem taught me to swim," Billy shouted over his shoulder, glancing back and forth between us and the road. "He was a year or two older than me. I used to follow him around in the holidays for a while. He stopped me shooting a kingfisher once. 'Don't kill what you don't need,' he said. He could catch a trout in his hand. I've seen him. He would have been a terrible poacher in years to come."

The lanes meandered to the sea and occasionally we stopped to allow wagons to pass us. Sometimes we sang, Jessica turning in her seat to conduct the chorus, 'One of the ruins that Cromwell knocked about a bit.' Other times, she leant against Billy, holding the brim of her hat back to whisper in his ear. When we took turns too fast, Constance's thigh pressed against mine as we slid on the leather seat.

We left the car and climbed to the top of a ridge of dunes. Below us was a beach that seemed to run for miles and was empty except for a far distant man with a dog. To the right, giant rocks left by the nearby crumbling cliff gave lots of cover for changing. As school freestyle champion and with a municipal lifesaving medal, I had my usual fantasy of rescuing companions from crashing surf but quickly realised that wouldn't happen. After hopping and splashing entries, shrieking at the cold of the sea compared with the heat of the sun on their backs, both Jessica and Constance, once immersed, set off with steady breast strokes straight out to sea, keeping their heads with their carefully pinned up hair out of the water. I set off energetically after them. Constance swam in a wide circle and returned to the beach. She sat on the sand with the waves rolling over her legs. I lay face down a yard out, being alternately swept in and dragged out, allowing the sun to beat down on my shoulders.

Constance leant back on her arms. Sleeves reached half way down to her elbows but the thin navy blue of her costume did little to preserve her modesty.

She folded her arms across the curve of her breasts and her nipples, cold from the sea, which had been fascinating me.

"Don't stare, George. It's embarrassing. Have you never seen a woman before?"

Gazing up at her serious face I searched my mind for a clever reply.

"No," I said with a candour that surprised me.

We all lay in the sun to dry ourselves until the hamper drew us to explore it. We shook salt onto hard boiled eggs, opened ginger beer bottles, crunched cucumber sandwiches.

"It's like a midnight feast in the dorm," Billy said and I agreed although I'd never attended one.

Jessica and Billy wandered off down the beach. Constance sighed as she gazed after them.

"Poor Billy."

"Poor Billy?"

"He and Jessica. It will never happen."

"Will Sir Richard forbid it?"

She laughed.

"Richard's a poppet despite his appearance. His bark's much worse than his bite. Hester has the voice that counts."

"I found Billy's father rather daunting."

Constance smiled.

"Young men do. I did once but you wouldn't if you saw him with Pippa. She takes him off on walks around the grounds and he listens to her very seriously. When she was five, he told her he'd found something magic outside that must be hers because it was her birthday and when we got there he'd hung all kinds of things from a gooseberry bush: chocolate money, doll's furniture, a brooch, a ribbon and things; all presents for her."

Constance wore her straw hat. Her chin rested on her raised knees and she was pouring sand over her feet as she said:

"Richard's very sweet. When Dicky was killed," she began. My heart sank. I found these conversations so trying, not knowing whether to sympathise miserably or try to jolly her out of it. "About three weeks later," she went on, "I wandered into the kitchen garden and found Richard just lighting a bonfire. I said, 'What on earth are you

49

doing?' and he looked so guilty and distraught that I pressed him on it when he wouldn't tell me and eventually he said, 'I'm going to burn Dicky's tunic.' I said 'Have you got Dicky's tunic? Where is it?' He wouldn't give it to me but of course, I had to see it. 'There's blood on it,' he said and there was. It seemed to be nothing but blood. It was stiff with blood. And it was in pieces from where they'd cut it off him and there were holes from the bullets. 'I can't let his mother see it,' Richard said. So we both burned Dicky's tunic."

Tears rolled down her cheeks.

"Why did they send it?"

"They sent all his things. I found the package in the hall. Richard had opened it and made off with the tunic. I still remember the smell of the kitbag and his spare clothes and my letters he'd kept. Everything was damp and muddy and had this damp, muddy smell like corruption and then I understood why Dicky took so much cologne back with him. He must have spent all his days out there with that terrible smell of corruption in his nostrils."

On this hot summer's day, on this English beach, despite our maudlin talk of corruption and dead men's effects, I knew I was immune from death, and more than that, my departure for the front was imminent and there were better things to do. I stood up.

"Would you like a walk?"

She rose and wiped her eyes with the handkerchief I'd rummaged through my clothes for.

"You're the first person I've told about Dicky's

tunic. No one knows it came back. Even Billy. You mustn't tell him. It would be too cruel for him."

We started off in the opposite direction to Billy and Jessica.

"I'm sorry to load you with my feelings, George. You must forgive me. I know it's not the thing to do. Women must send men off with smiles on their faces. But you listen so well. You make it all spill out. Most people never listen. They're waiting for a pause to introduce their own story. You feel very wise to me for someone so young. Oh, and I know that you'll be back. From France, I mean. I have this feeling."

I felt quite cheered, splashing next to Constance through the shallows; pleased with her and pleased with me; rewarded for my pains. I was wise, a good listener and would have a safe return.

In the cottage garden which we stopped at for tea, Billy made an announcement.

"We're to be engaged, Jessica and I."

"Are you going to tell your mother and father?" Constance asked immediately.

"Of course. We want it all settled before I leave."

"Hester was pleased when Billy wrote to say he was bringing you," Constance had told me as we paddled on the sea's edge. "She thought you might distract Jessica."

The idea had made me laugh out loud.

"I don't think I'd distract anyone from Billy," I said.

"Incessant charm can pall, George," she said.

In the bath later, I still could not quite believe that Billy might not be constantly and universally liked, least of all by his sister-in-law, and quickly dismissed the absurd thought that she might perhaps resent that Billy was alive and his brother, her husband, dead.

Dinner that evening was less grand but it was clear that the meat rationing which so affected my mother and father in London had not quite extended to the countryside or at least to the people who owned most of it. Cold roast chicken was served with new boiled potatoes and peas cooked with sprigs of mint. Jessica, if invited, was not present. Perhaps she was leaving the coast clear for Billy or perhaps after her day's holiday, she had to prepare for her return in the morning to the hospital she nursed at.

After dinner, we went to the billiard room. Sir Richard's cigar smoke hung in layers below the light above the table. Billy showed me snooker first.

"More balls than in billiards, you must hit something," he said. Sir Richard found it mildly alarming that I could have reached my age and never played the game.

"It's all angles and things, where you strike the ball and where you aim on the cushion for the rebound," Billy explained. "It's a bit like deflection shooting in the air."

To hit a target towed by an aeroplane as it flew across in front of you, it was necessary to aim at the aeroplane, which took an act of faith, by shooter and shot at.

Snooker proved irritating but not impossible. As Billy passed on his way to the wall rack to pick up a rest, he said quietly, "Go for a walk after this frame, George. You know," then went on, "you're next Pa, when I've beaten George."

I left them to it. In the sitting room, Constance looked up from *Vogue*. Behind her, through the window, darkness had almost fallen. The prospect of a later moonlit stroll gave our smiles a silent conspiratorial feel. I sank into the sofa and picked up *The Times*. Lady Love was elsewhere and Constance and I smiled again.

"Billy's talking to Sir Richard."

Constance grimaced and hunched her shoulders.

I rustled through the casualty lists and checked for three of my school fellows I knew to be at the front. They'd had another lucky day but as my eye moved automatically down it spotted: "McCudden, JTB Maj. RAF, VC, DSO and Bar, MC and Bar, MM, Croix de Guerre".

I remember the shock of sudden insecurity that stabbed through me. If the Hun had got McCudden, our peerless pilot, what would they not do to Billy and me? As a pilot, I could barely keep formation in the air. I lit a cigarette and imagined McCudden's bloodstained tunic on its way home. Or perhaps he was burnt and there was no tunic left on his charred corpse. Then I found an article. Not the Hun, an elementary flying error! He'd turned back to the field after his engine cut out on take off. It was as bad as Keble's mistake.

I laid aside *The Times* and filled my mind with tune titles as I went through the pile of records, then occupied my hands winding the gramophone and placing the needle. I walked to the window and stared at the as yet moonless black outside but saw only the reflection of the room; armchair, settee, lamps, Constance, as the absurd words, so divorced from bodies burning or tumbling through emptiness, broke the hiss.

And when I tell them how beautiful you are.
They'll never believe me, they'll never believe me.

I kept my back to Constance as we listened together. My confidence was truly shaken by McCudden's death. For the first time really, I could imagine my own bloodstained tunic coming home to my mother, she who had so stoically accepted my too brief stay on embarkation leave.

The record finished.

"Dicky liked that song. 'They'll never believe me'," Constance said.

There was the loud bang of a door from the direction of the billiard room. We heard rapid steps through the hall and the creak and slam of the main door.

Constance rose and led me outside.

"They didn't believe him," she said.

We progressed slowly along the paths and through the trees, stopping to look at the peacocks behind their fox-proof wire. Constance was affectionate again.

Alone in my room, after we'd said goodnight, I listened for Billy's return until I decided I wouldn't hear him anyway, isolated as I was in this room at the far west end of the house. I lay in the dark on the stripped back bed, hot even in just the legs of the cotton pyjamas my mother had bought me at 6d a week.

Wide awake still, I imagined burning aeroplanes and my charred corpse among the embers. Finally, anxious to sleep, I stared through the open window at the moon. I forced myself to listen to the absolute singing silence of the countryside, and sensed again the soft round give of Constance's breast against my hand through her dress as we lingered in the dark beneath the trees. I had progressed to wondering how the flesh would feel to my hand when there was a tap at the door.

I sat up, imagining Billy outside wanting a cigarette and a sympathetic ear but it was Constance who slid in and locked the door. She looked at me in the moonlight for an instant. Her long dark hair fell past her shoulders and the silk robe tied tightly around her shone. She came and sat beside me.

"I'm so lonely, George," she said and slipped my hand inside her robe.

I can't believe my performance was more than perfunctory. I'd never seen a naked woman before and such was my excitement that more than three-quarters of a century on it's still easy to imagine the grand thrilling shock of her bare flesh against mine. But Constance perhaps had low expectations. I believe there were sighs and gasps and at some point I could have sworn I heard a peacock crying. Then there were embraces and sleep until I woke to a lightening room as Constance rose and pulled on her robe, kissed me and left.

I was still hot and remembered the scent and softness of Constance so strongly that I could sleep no more. I put on a shirt and trousers and crept downstairs to the terrace and then to the grass, which dampened my shoes with the dew of dawn. The cool air refreshed me and cleared my mind. For a moment I remembered Billy and wondered where he'd been and what time he'd come back. Then the cataclysmic look and feel of Constance's naked body returned and I realised I couldn't now leave for a sudden short visit to my poor rejected mother as had crossed my mind the evening before. In fact, I wished I had more than one more night to spend in this wonderful house.

I'd entered the trees and was going back towards the house when I saw through the wire of the enclosure a peacock sleeping on its side. I thought this very curious until I got closer and I saw that it wasn't sleeping. Then I understood what the cries I'd heard during the night had been. I saw the throat askew and feathers, now dull with no sunlight or movement to make them shimmer, scattered around the mauled carcase. Amongst the feathers, awful purple-pink organs and intestines ripped by the fox from this dazzling exotic bird lay jumbled and splattered across the earth of the enclosure.

Three

There's a photograph, much reprinted in books on the subject, from one of which I tore it years ago, whose caption reads, "Somewhere in France, SE5s prepare for patrol." Several points about the picture prove the caption wrong though.

Nine SEs are visible but we usually did patrols in flights of six. The hangars are permanent English ones, not the canvas ones used in France. The aeroplanes, spruced up for review, shine even in the monochrome of the photo. Pilots stand about in cocky groups, ready for an outing. Even the mechanics are not the dishevelled zombies that endless hours of work in France often turned them into but smiling craftsmen, crisp and ready for their tasks; to swing a propeller, to pull away chocks. The lie is finally shown by the letters on the fuselages which reveal that the immaculate biplanes have been lined up carefully in alphabetical order. And in fact I know the caption errs. I remember the photographer setting up his tripod on a platform before we took off to fly to France.

If this image goes on down through history, we will

remain as captured in time as the figures Keats writes of in his Ode. *What men or gods are these?* Well, on this Grecian urn of ours Mitch will forever sit in machine 'A', goggles up, propeller invisible and engine roar silent as he tests it one last time; and the warm sun of that morning will continue to cast the shadows of Butcher, Baker, Billy and myself, helmeted and flying-suited, as we grin our bravado at the camera. Minutes later, our machines bounced and rattled as we tore across the field in three's until all shocks ceased and we soared and sank and soared again over the trees and turned, engines snarling, to gain formation. Only five machines of 'C' Flight joined us. Someone had not got off and now either stood cursing his engine or lay smashed and bleeding in the wreckage.

We climbed across Southern England. Above was a gigantic blue vault, smudged here and there with white, home to the huge yellow dazzle of the sun. Below lay the usual ravishing patchwork colours: the green and gold of fields, the russet of woods, the red and grey of roofs, the grey-black of ribbon-like roads, the silver snakes of rivers, all bright and shining in the sun until dulled on occasions by the enormous shadows of passing clouds. A thin line of grey smoke cut through this landscape and travelled parallel with us. A week ago we might have dived and raced the train but not today. Germans, whose land I'd never seen but which could only be less gentle, less refined that ours, wanted all this; our home. Our serious business today, which would not allow us to race the train, was to defend the sublime tidiness below.

But it was still a jaunt so far. There was nothing to do but keep formation, enjoy the view and eat one's chocolate, which I saw Billy doing fifty yards across from me. As his machine rose and fell slightly in relation to mine, he raised his hand to offer some to me. He could always make me laugh, even when he was feeling low, as he was the day I found the peacock.

"Dear, dear," Billy said, looking at the carnage with me. "Ma and Pa will be upset. But it serves them right. They said hateful things about Jess."

I had a sudden vision of a vengeful Billy kneeling in the dark, digging away in a frenzy at the earth below the wire, making a tunnel with his bare hands for the fox he knew would find it, when I had imagined him somewhere shadowed, weeping for his dashed hopes. But his nails were as immaculate as ever. Had he used a spade?

"Where did you go last night?" I said.

"I wanted to see Jess but the house was dark. I went to the barn I used to play in and thought about dropping my cigarette there and costing them hundreds. But then I thought, 'Don't be a fool. It'll all be yours anyway. You can do what you like next year'."

"When you're twenty-one, you mean?"

"Yes."

"But mightn't they cut you off if they disapprove so much?"

"Their only surviving son?"

"Well?"

"I can't live a prisoner of the nineteenth century, George. It's them who'll have to change. It's votes for

59

women now and Bolshevism too if we don't watch out."

He made it sound a terrifying prospect as we stared at the entrails of that aristocratic peacock.

"Come on," Billy said, "let's have breakfast. What about some kidneys?" I groaned and laughed for a moment. He guided me towards the house.

"If I'm turned away from the ancestral home, we can start a joy ride business. Ten bob a flip – fifty bob an hour, how's that?"

Of course, I thought, as we crossed the terrace towards the dining room doors, whatever happened to Billy's inheritance, I would still have the problem of what to do after the war. Supposing I was still alive as Constance had assured me I would be. And where would Constance figure post war?

"I shall write," she'd said, "if I may."

"Oh, please," I said. I was unsure of the etiquette required. Our courtship had been swift and secret and my sexual education swifter and yet more secret. In the days after I left her it was an experience my mind would settle on immediately the demands of war allowed it. And a flight across Southern England allowed it.

Although I didn't see a naked Constance dancing through the rigging wires, again and again I imagined the smooth curve of her hip and thigh, the concentration on her face in the moonlight, her closed eyes and her wonderful warm tightness as I entered her. Imagination made me yearn for her even, or perhaps especially, in the chill air of ten thousand feet.

Yes, she would write and I'd answer and more could not be done in the limbo of war.

A Sopwith Camel flew up and stunted around beside us, hoping to entice one or two of us to play. When the pilot realised he couldn't persuade anyone, he did a final roll in salute and dived away. We descended, too, as the sea came into sight and the coast of France twenty miles away. We landed for lunch and to top up our tanks. There were sausages of a strange flavour. After a cigarette, I had to find a latrine quickly where I vomited again and again. The sausage or the war, I wondered? After a glass of water I felt better.

We put on life jackets, took off again and crossed the cliffs at Dover, lining up on the two white markers a quarter of a mile apart that gave the bearing for the shortest crossing. The sea sparkled. We overtook a white-waked transport with three weaving anti-submarine destroyer escorts and suddenly we were crossing breakers on a beach and were over France.

Still in sunshine, we landed at our new home: a large field with farm buildings to which the RAF had added huts and canvas hangars. By the side of one of these was a makeshift tennis court. Four players looked up from their doubles match as we flew over. The major was there to greet us. Our fitters and riggers helped us out and fussed around the machines they hadn't seen for days.

We gathered in groups and looked about us. France from the air had looked less neat than England. We'd seen army camps, a large hospital with red crosses in huge white squares on the roof and much railway traffic but apart from the odd marching column and a few khaki trucks, little sign of active war. Then the final engine stopped and I became aware of a distant rumble. I looked at Baker.

"Guns," he said.

Sweltering now in the sun, we pulled off flying suits and lit cigarettes.

"Tea this way, chaps," the major called.

Billy came over, grinning. Then we heard rotary engines. Above the trees half a mile away, three Camels appeared. We watched them touch down and taxi to their sheds on the far side of the field. Their engines stopped but the sound did not. From beyond the trees came another rotary engine, less robust, missing on one cylinder. Another Camel appeared flying slightly sideways as if blown by a wind. The engine stopped. The Camel touched down and bounced and bounced again. "I'm glad someone else does it," I was thinking when the right wing touched the grass and the machine slewed round, raising dust from the dry ground. It completed half a circle and finished tipped up on its nose facing the trees it had flown over. The pilot didn't move. Figures started to run from the sheds opposite. An ambulance started up.

"Someone caught a packet," Baker said.

"Tea up, you blokes," Mitch called, "Come on."

I followed, watching over my shoulder, as I saw Billy did too. Four men struggled to pull the pilot from the wreck. They carried him on his back at shoulder height for a few yards. He was bulky in his flying suit and his unsupported head hung down. As his bearers laid him gently on the earth, his goggles caught the sun. The flash I saw seemed to me disturbingly like a warning.

It had been an exhausting day. Mitch planned an early show to see the lines so I went to bed when darkness fell. There was no sign of Billy in the bare wooden hut I was sharing with him. I fell asleep at once but woke after only minutes according to my watch. I could hear traffic and soldiers singing. I sat up and lit a candle. The door opened and Billy's face looked round it.

"Come and see the war, George!"

I pulled on trousers and boots and tunic. The noise increased as I followed Billy to the bank above the road that skirted the airfield only fifty yards from our huts. Officers lined the bank. Below us, the dimmed headlights of occasional trucks revealed men in rumpled khaki marching three abreast on their way up to the lines. They had rifles slung on shoulders, helmets hanging on huge packs, caps set at jaunty angles. Sometimes they marched in silence, bright pinpricks of cigarettes in their mouths, sometimes raucous, obscene songs drowned the sound of their feet on the stones of the road. Huge artillery pieces with enormous rumbling wheels and giant barrels, pulled by chugging tractors, filled the spaces between the groups of infantry. The headlamps of a tractor would play a yellow light on the gun in front, casting bizarre and ghastly shadows, making the gun seem truly an engine of death.

"God help Fritz," Billy said.

"Bugger Fritz," I heard Butcher say from the dark to my right. "I hope they blow him to hell."

I dragged myself away eventually and lay in the hut. Flying had altered the military habits of centuries. Aeroplanes were the eyes of the army but after dark the eyes were blind. To preserve some tactical advantage, troops now had to move at night.

The noise continued. It was the same all through my time in France and naturally I came to ignore it but that night I couldn't sleep again and blamed the engines and the songs, not admitting it was fears of tomorrow's flight that made me lie awake. Of course, as I lay motionless and pretended sleep when Billy came in and quietly got to bed, those fears returned in waves. What would it be like to be shot at; from the ground by Archie, in the air by Spandau machine guns? Would I keep my head in a turning match with a Fokker, like the one I'd had with Mitch? We were just going to look tomorrow, I told myself. There was nothing to frighten me. Why couldn't I lie sleeping easily like Billy, from whom no sound came?

Our look the next day was fine in fact, a mere quiet outing over our own territory, as were others on following days. Our first real job a week later, though, was a very strange and unsettling experience. I was right to have fears and the really worrying part was something I hadn't at all anticipated.

We took off at seven. Mitch climbed in wide circles, showing us the land around the field again so that we could pick out from the air the landmarks we'd noted on our maps. Height was safety and Mitch didn't want to cross the lines below sixteen thousand feet. When we reached that height, we turned east and continued climbing, growing progressively colder. I had my hands full juggling with the throttle to stay in formation. Large white clouds shared the sky with us and far below the ground slowly turned from the colours of cultivation to a uniform pitted brown. It reminded me immediately of the floor of the rhinoceros pen at Regent's Park Zoo. As a boy I'd once stood in the rain under an umbrella, waiting for my mother, and watched that huge pacing animal squelch and pound the grassless earth into mud. It was the front lines exactly.

Without warning, in the sky ahead of me to the right, what seemed like a large black bear appeared. It was woolly and shaggy and it barked a loud 'wumpf' at me over the noise of the engine. As it spread itself out and dispersed, two more bears appeared to my right and two more 'wumpfs' barked. Although Mitch had warned us about Archie, unconsciously I jerked the machine away from the shell bursts. We were being fired at from the ground. I steeled myself and kicked the SE back into formation. Butcher and Baker and Leigh, the dead Keble's replacement had not moved from their positions but I noticed Billy also pulling back into the formation.

More woolly black bears "wumpfed" around us. I could easily imagine what they might do to wood and canvas. Mitch began a gentle dive and we followed. After a few seconds he zoomed. The black bears appeared where we would have been. We went on our way, diving and zooming, turning and straightening. I was pleased to have Mitch to lead the dance for on my own I felt I might have found myself diving away. Finally the shelling stopped. That was a sign of enemy aircraft I'd been told, so as we flew up and down the lines between banks of clouds, I stared around as taught and raised my thumb against the sun to protect my eyes from dazzle. We were alone in the sky I decided. I wasn't disappointed. Archie must just have got tired.

After three quarters of an hour, we turned west and started a descent. I began to think the worst was over. Then Mitch raised an arm and his machine disappeared. I put the nose down and followed. My ears popped. Mitch pulled up but too quickly for me. The flight was scattered. I stuck with Baker. We circled and then suddenly Mitch and the others were there again.

We made for home. I concentrated on remembering my lessons and throttled back to put the machine down at just the right speed. The SE settled and didn't bounce. We pulled up at the hangars and I slowly got out. My legs were trembling I remember. I leant against the fuselage and wondered how the others felt but knew they'd never tell me. I looked up. There was a crowd around Mitch. I kicked my insecure legs towards them.

"Bloody good, Mitch," I heard Billy say. People were slapping Mitch's back.

"What's up?" I asked Billy quietly.

"The two-seater Mitch shot down." My face must have been a picture.

"Didn't you see it, George?" Billy laughed.

"I say, you chaps!" Billy called excitedly. "George didn't see it. George didn't see Mitch's two-seater. How abso-bloody-lutely priceless!"

Everyone fell about laughing, Mitch most of all. Then he put his arm around my shoulder and led me off to report.

"Tell me, George, honour bright, did you really not see it?"

"Not a sausage."

He told me all about it.

After crossing the lines, it seemed Mitch had spotted a dozen Fokkers. Since it was our first time over, he'd decided we should avoid them, which we did by playing hide and seek in the clouds. Then for twenty minutes we'd tracked a two-seater Rumpler engaged in photo-reconnaissance. Mitch had dived and pulled up beneath the Rumpler to shoot it down. He'd watched it fall on our side of the lines.

I was appalled.

"It happens to lots of fellows first time over," Mitch said. "You'll see them tomorrow."

It was a great day, the squadron's first victory and after breakfast we would all drive to find the wreckage. Mitch wanted a machine gun to take home to his girl.

The major lent the squadron car, with orders not to crash it. Baker and Butcher stayed behind. Baker's engine was missing and he wanted to test it. Butcher had seen enough trenches and wrecked aeroplanes. He would look up acquaintances in the Camel squadron across the field. Billy drove. If there was a steering wheel available, he always wanted to be behind it.

Leigh and I sat in the back and leant forward to join the conversation. Leigh was a dark-haired, serious young chap from Nottingham. When you spoke to him, he'd stare at you, thinking deeply before replying, usually with a soft smile. He was another of us driven by Albert Ball's example but whereas mine was newspaper knowledge, he remembered a shy, dignified young man whom he sometimes spotted in the streets of their native city. One day in 1916 when Ball was home on leave, Leigh had come upon him broken down at the roadside and helped him to put the chain back on his motor-cycle. Ball was softly spoken and polite Leigh said, which confirmed the major's impressions.

They'd served in neighbouring squadrons and the major, then a lieutenant, had often popped into the hut Ball had built from packing cases by the side of the hangar his Nieuport biplane was kept in. Ball had made a garden around his hut in which to rest from the war and killing Germans by growing vegetables for the mess. Ball kept his distance but he was shy, the major said, not stand-offish. When his gramophone wasn't playing, they heard him practising his violin. 'Humoresque' by Dvorak was his party piece. All callers were welcome to join him in a deckchair among the cabbages and carrots. Ball had been dead more than a year. With his lone warrior, Royal Flying Corps ways, he would not perhaps have fitted into the RAF's new, more organised approach to fighting. We now flew and fought as formations and flight leaders stalked and pounced on the enemy rather than diving hell for leather into their midst whatever the odds, as Ball had done.

Mitch called out the directions he'd received on the phone from the Archie battery which had witnessed the fall of his two-seater. We passed increasing dereliction: villages, where not a building remained whole, and chimney breasts emerged from piles of rubble; splintered stumps of trees that had once formed shady copses; cratered earth as far as the eye could see. We were immediately behind the old front line. Shirt sleeved gunners in this destroyed landscape waved to us as they lugged shells into piles. Not far from the road, an observation balloon hovered on its moorings twenty feet above its basket, which was tethered to the ground. We pulled up to watch the balloon's observer, the lucky man, strap a parachute on. Unlike pilots of the RAF, all balloon observers were equipped with them.

The Archie battery commander, a captain, like Mitch, slopped celebratory tots of whisky into tin mugs. He was full of admiration for Mitch's victory. Archie gunners spent their days scanning the sky with binoculars. They were connoisseurs of air fights and Mitch's, with its quick dive, pull up and short burst of fire, had had the economic simplicity of a classic. Pilot and observer had been found dead in their seats. The pilot was a sergeant, the observer an officer, a common German arrangement. They lay grey and stiff under a tarpaulin. Anxious how I would react, I pretended to myself that they were waxworks and didn't linger over them. Mitch said we should arrange a squadron escort for their funerals.

The captain led us to the wreck. For him this little trip was a distraction from the daily round but for Mitch, Billy, Leigh and I it was a tourist excursion to the ground war. The captain was our guide and gave out information, warned of dangers. Here the line had held for months. This trench the Guards had taken with bomb and bayonet. Beware of snipers here. We gawped as sightseers do who can return to comfortable hotels, as we could to the squadron and our deckchairs in the sun. Inquisitive, we peered at the inhabitants of this world, the poor bloody infantry, as they went about their daily round of eating, washing, defecating, writing letters, cleaning their kit and weapons, repairing their abodes with sandbags. Then we left them crouching below their parapets and squatting on fire steps surrounded by depravity and squalor while they breathed in that dank, indescribable, ever present smell that Constance had recognised as corruption.

These were support trenches that we were moving through, taken only recently from the Germans. Their situation on a gentle hillside had given good views and fields of fire onto the old British positions. The British line now sat on the top of the rise. We saw wreckage to the right, a mass of crumpled wood and fabric which lay in the dead ground protected by the rise ahead. We scrambled up to the wreck and Mitch got busy with the hacksaw he'd brought along. We had little time to admire the sight for our guide said that when the enemy balloons we could see three or four miles away spotted us, the Germans would shell the wreck.

Mitch tore his trophy free and we, his acolytes and supporters, scurried off behind him. I remember being pleased for him. Mitch was a constant inspiration and a calmer down of nerves. He was a colonial and the best of them, though I loved all the colonials I met in the service: Canadians, South Africans, Australians, New Zealanders; and so did Billy. They were cheery and open and friendly. They'd come across the world to fight for Britain. They had a sense of adventure. With them all things seemed possible. With them it was always what you did that mattered, not who you were. Much later, I heard of a squadron that hadn't wanted McCudden to command them because as the son of a corporal, born in barracks, he wasn't their sort. My colonial friends would have laughed. Billy would have seethed.

"I hate snobbery," he said one day as he lolled in a deckchair in the sun outside our hut, his tunic off, his khaki braces hanging down, one long leg crossed over the other, a cigarette dangling from loose fingers. I responded in the style of the sixth form debating society I hadn't long left.

"What do you mean by snobbery?"

"Why, the thought that any single human being is inherently better than any other."

"That sounds like socialism."

"No. Common sense and humanity."

Suddenly languid no more, Billy sat forward on the

chair, feet firmly planted, eyes ablaze, elbows on knees but fingers extended, hands gesticulating.

"Look at us George. Grammar school and Eton. But here we are together in deckchairs in France, both with the same commissions, waiting to kill the King's Germans for him. How can one of us be better than the other? It isn't socialism. We're equal. We're the same. And we should be thought of as the same."

He pushed his hair back with that characteristic flick.

After the war I found most politicians stale fare compared with Billy. He would have been captivating on an election platform and would have fixed a crowd with that voice and those eyes. He would have made an immediate impact and despite his non-socialist claims, the Tories might have found it tough to keep him in their fold till he was old enough to develop a benevolent paternalism of the Macmillan kind.

His parents, moreover, though they didn't know it, were fanning a democratic flame in him that I still fancy might have had political results but for the war.

"My people seem to think Jessica is beneath me," he said that day in France. "It's monstrous. She's a human being, breathes and eats like all of us. She's clever, educated, sings and draws and rides. What more can they want?"

"Someone your sort, I suppose."

"My sort!"

"Someone titled. Someone whose brother went to Eton."

"Eton! Eton, George, and Ma knows it, is full of

Viscounts, Earls, Marquises, Dukes and Indian princes. They wouldn't normally pass the time of day with the Lady of a dowdy baronet, you know. They might well treat her the way she treats Jessica. They treated me like that often enough, her son."

He put on a voice.

"'How many acres does you father have, Love?' Looking down their noses. God's teeth! People can be appalling. And my people worst of all. Thank God for Canadians, I say. That's the way things will be after the war; the way they do things. Everyone should have his chance. Let everyone achieve what he can. Fair dos all round, I say."

Back in the mess, Mitch put his machine gun as a centrepiece on our lunch table and everyone gawked at it. In the afternoon I wandered over to the sheds. I went around the back for a cigarette with my fitter, Johnson. A hundred yards away across a field was a small deciduous wood.

"Looks like Kent, doesn't it, sir? You've never been hopping, I suppose."

I hadn't but I had put a bicycle in the guard's van to Bromley South and ridden along lanes around Westerham, where General Wolfe was born and where, later, Churchill lived, and I had freewheeled down the leaf-covered hills whooping my exhilaration in the wind that tore at my lungs.

"It does look like Kent here," I said, "apart from no hedges."

"Enclosures, sir. It's what took the land from the

common man. And we got hedges instead." My history was not strong enough to argue with him. Johnson was a year or two older. He spoke well with me using the accent four years at grammar school had given him but I knew he slid out of it easily when I left him and would double negatives, drop aitches and eff and blind with his mates and the flight sergeant.

"Wouldn't you like to learn to fly, Johnson? Get a commission?" I said voicing the thought I'd had several times. "I'm sure the major would put you up for one." He looked at me as if about to laugh.

"No thanks, sir. Not likely. My father's only a cobbler. I don't want to go getting above myself. Of course, he's always got a book in his hands and he's made us all into readers, too, sir."

"But more money, Johnson, more standing," I said, expressing the unworthy feelings I myself had.

"You may be right, sir, but as far as standing goes, if anyone has a problem with the Wolseley, it's me they send for, sir. And as for money," Johnson went on, for he was never so churlish as to let silence speak for him, "I've enough for now and my Dolly, she's on munitions work, sir, and putting some aside for later. She wants me back in one piece." Thus he put me neatly in my place. Money's no use to you in your box he was saying.

Men like Johnson, though valued less highly in terms of pay, were in reality as essential as we pilots, who mistreated the engines and airframes they cared for so conscientiously.

"I thank my lucky stars I got into engines when I

did, sir, before the war. There's not many better than me, though I says it as shouldn't." He laughed and trod out his cigarette stub.

"We'll be nicely set, Dolly and me," he waved a thumb towards the rumbling guns, "when all this is over. There'll be good businesses in aviation. Let's just hope we all get through in one piece."

I was pleased to be included in his wish for good fortune and I could sense the pity he regarded me with. He had to work all hours in trying conditions and he did it with a will, but it was me who went up to be shot at, me who'd been duped into patriotic fervour.

But at least that had given me a wonderful toy to play with, my SE. I went up to stunt off my irritation. I've found that flight in my log book. An area familiarisation I called it. I have the log book in front of me now. An hour of non-war flying in just goggles, since I wouldn't go above the three thousand feet I reached in about four minutes, climbing along the road that led towards the roofs of Amiens, ten miles away. I always felt delightfully free and uncramped in the SE's cockpit when I flew without gauntlets and heavy flying suit. The wind would flow through my hair, though as my ears grew colder, I'd always slowly regret the absent helmet.

As I write this now, I also have a Michelin map for reference, so I know that over Talmas I might well have banked towards the Front until I reached the triangular wood at Toutencourt. Thus I would dutifully have quartered the area and noted again the woods and railway lines, crossroads, villages and towns

I'd seen that morning; Belle Eglise, Louvencourt, Beauquesne, Terramesnil. When I was flying back from the line, these were the landmarks that would guide me home.

Then, duty done, I'm sure I rolled to left and right, swooped down again and contour-chased across fields of wheat to pull up over roadside trees at the last moment, keenly aware of the high-pitched snarl of the engine now undampened by a helmet. I'd have banked on a wing tip fifty feet above the ground and chased lorries up the road to Puchevillers. Then above Montplaisir, I met Baker on his engine test. I made a note of it in my logbook. We undoubtedly played follow my leader, looping, rolling, turning, chasing each other along the river towards Doullens till he gave the time for home signal and I hedge-hopped after him beside the Amiens road back to the airfield, ravenous for tea, with my humour restored.

When I came into the hut, Billy was occupying the table, preventing me from writing to my mother. I flopped on the bed.

"What a pick me up flying is," I said.

"No Archie?" Billy asked.

We laughed.

"God! What wind up! For two pins I'd have flown home."

It was always safe to claim wind up when your actions clearly showed the opposite. That morning I'd flown unseeing through a battle. My blindness had gained me a certain standing in the squadron.

"Logbook?" I asked, nodding at what Billy was writing.

"My diary," he said.

"What? Sun shining? Toast for breakfast?"

"That sort of thing. It's very interesting to look back at the days you've lived through."

"I've never had the patience. I admire you for it." In fact Billy had surprised me. I wouldn't have taken him for a diarist.

"You must write something," he said and turned to the back pages. There were inscriptions in different coloured inks and different scripts.

"If we are what we think we are, what are we?" I read, signed "Lt. H. Thomas May 27 1918" and "Cheery O. Roger Gibson 24. 5. 18."

"Don't let your wires sing. Capt. N. Coe RAF 2. 4. 18" and "Times change and we with them but, NOT in the way of Friendship. A. Gower."

Under one or two Billy had added a postscript in his own hand,

"Killing spinning, Apr. 4th '18." "Killed in air fight, France June 7th '18." "Missing May 25th '18."

"I'm not sure I want to write anything," I said. "Is it safe?"

"Come on, George, a keepsake."

I thought hard, as you do, hoping not to disappoint, trying to avoid embarrassment as the owner of the book waits to read your thoughts. Eventually I remembered an oddity gleaned from *The Times* a few days before, which pleases me now much more that it did then.

"The left-handed salute has been abolished. I never knew it existed.

George Bridge RAF 18/7/18".

The writing of the person I was then was more ornate; looped and whorled like finger prints. I used Billy's fountain pen and I still have it somewhere. That page is before me now. Billy's diary has helped me reconstruct my memory. I must be the only signatory still drawing breath.

Butcher returned that evening with an invitation for 'A' flight to join the Camel squadron for dinner. It was to be a binge. One of their flight commanders was going home, always a cause for celebration, and his DFC was through, another reason. It was the pilot we'd seen lifted from his wrecked machine. He'd been thoroughly shot up from the ground but had been merely a little concussed in the crash. He had half a dozen Huns but more importantly from a novice pilot's viewpoint prided himself that he'd never been surprised by enemy aircraft and, probably a unique achievement, had never lost a member of his flight to a Hun pilot. His followers all quite rightly revered him, Butcher said, and were anxious over his departure, since they would now have to fend for themselves after three months with "Auntie", as they called him.

Billy's diary reminds me there was pate and veal and a burgundy that was halfway good, Billy says, but Mitch had warned us for an early job, so we couldn't do it justice. This was an aspect of squadron life that would become a pattern; a comfortable almost luxurious life with danger and death a short flight away, like a migraine aura at the corner of your vision.

The guest of honour sat beaming, as well he might. His forehead was cut and both eyes were still yellow and blue from his crash. It seemed to me that he wasn't altogether sure what was going on, though whether as a result of concussion still or merely alcohol I couldn't be sure. Several people, including his major and a colonel from wing made speeches saying what a jolly good fellow he was. It seemed infinitely enviable to be a hero having won the right to a hero's return wearing a Distinguished Flying Cross ribbon. Meanwhile we had our migraine auras of danger and death still at the corners of our vision. The job next morning was to escort a squadron of De Havilland 9s to bomb the rail junction at Rozieres, ten miles across the lines. A quick dash of five minutes to the target but ten minutes back against the prevailing west wind which was the almost constant second enemy we battled.

That night, while Billy lay still and slept, I lay awake and called up Fokkers to distress me. Grey-faced waxworks flew them in combat scenarios which simulated attacks from above, below, behind and the side. I would twist and peer round in my cockpit to prevent the enemy from pouncing on me unseen and instantly turn towards them before they could stitch bullets across my back.

In the mess at four, my eyes stung from lack of sleep as we silently ate our eggs and drank our tea. Through the windows, the hangars were dark mounds just becoming visible. One by one the engines of our

SEs coughed, exploded and burst into life as the fitters ran them up, drowning out 'Danny Boy', that someone had just put on the gramophone to cover the rumble of the dawn bombardment. Mitch stood by the window imperturbable and strangely inspiring despite the mundane tea cup in his hand, until he lowered the cup and waved us all out. There was a promise of heat and it was in fact the last mainly fine day before the weather broke and gave us the conditions so difficult for flying that marked my time in France.

I waddled out in my kit. Dew would have formed on the wings and the padded leather cockpit rim I swung my leg over before wriggling into my seat and feeling the machine seem to give to accommodate me. Johnson was his usual cheery self, sending me off into the danger he had quite reasonably and honourably opted out of.

We bounced away from the hangars across the grass and took off in pairs, thirty yards apart. I felt my usual thrill of fear as the machine rose and sank and I wondered as always if this time it would fail to rise again. But it did rise of course and we were soon climbing along the Amiens road to meet the Nines as they circled over their field at Bertangles. From three thousand feet, the sun was already a clean orb above the eastern horizon.

We flew between the Nines, who were three thousand feet below us, and 'B' Flight led by Glover, who were five thousand feet above. Crossing the lines was much more comfortable today since the Nines drew all the Archie. They flew in three solid wedge formations and shells burst brown and black all around them. Although I pitied them, I felt like singing with relief. I was still very tense though and I constantly looked up and down and banked to see below the wings that blocked my view, twisting my neck to look behind, determined not to be caught napping. At the same time I was closely watching Mitch and Baker, on whom I was holding formation, and listening for the slightest change in the engine's roar that might signal a problem and leave me with a long anxious glide back alone through Archie to our lines. Then Mitch rocked his wings. I stared around the sky with added concentration and saw black dots against a large white cloud further ahead over Hunland.

In this situation I would always suddenly become even more anxious. The balls of my feet would begin to prickle and my toes to grow warm. The dots now had thin lines above and below them and were diving at us from a couple of miles away. Below my cockpit rim the Nines were still cruising on.

The Archie had stopped and the dots were crosses now and making for the Nines. I cocked my guns and glanced behind to check no other Huns had eluded 'B' Flight. The crosses became aeroplanes whose upper wings were longer than the lower ones. The sun flashed off their surfaces. Fokker biplanes, the first Germans I'd seen. There were half a dozen of them, hoping to reach the Nines with a dive before we caught them.

Mitch dropped his nose and I opened the throttle as he began to pull away. After my embarrassment of the day before, I had orders to stick close to him. I was pleased to do so since I knew that Mitch was calculating speeds and distances, angles, risks and chances but was also bearing my safety in mind as a small though vital element in his calculations, so the sight of the back of his head helped to quell the panic that was bubbling deep inside me.

I would have swallowed to clear my ears as the Fokkers grew in size. They were painted fairground colours. If it was to frighten us, it certainly worked with me.

Fear was an emotion we lived with daily. It was always there in prospect before we flew because in the air so many things could kill us: mechanical failure, Archie, machine guns, flames. Fear was like an incubus which you squashed deep in your gut as you took off and juggled controls and concentrated on map reading and maintaining formation. But an instant of danger would release it from its hidey hole to occupy all parts of your body to fight your will and conscience for possession of your faculties. It was a struggle that everyone in combat had and not every will, not even the greatest, always defeated its devil. In her biography of the Iron Duke, Elizabeth Longford describes a panic in a night attack in India which had Arthur Wellesley fleeing with his troops in the dark, the same Wellington who rode calmly through shot and shell at Waterloo.

In our dive that day, I struggled against possession by my incubus until the first of two things happened that helped me realise my fear would not completely master me. One of the rear Fokkers changed direction and showed the unpainted underside of its wings as it turned and dived for earth. Spotting us in the superior position, and probably also 'B' Flight perched above, that pilot, rationally perhaps or perhaps out of pure funk, had dived away to safety. I understood then that these warriors with war paint on their buses had wind up that was just as bad as mine.

We snarled down on open throttles to catch the Fokkers from the side. They were attacking from the front-right quarter, a difficult shot for the Nines' observers, forward over the wings and the pilot's head. Then all the Nines as one turned and climbed to face the attack head on. A Fokker flashed across in front of me, yellow and purple, too fast for me and I fired uselessly when it had gone. I banked left and followed Mitch, the sky on my right, the earth on my left. We were under the bombers now and Mitch was after a Fokker with a blue tail which pulled up vertically in front of us, then tipped to the right and fell into a spin. Mitch had pulled up too and his SE filled my windscreen. If I'd been a German, he would have been cold meat. I kicked left rudder sharply to avoid a collision and as I crossed just twenty feet above and behind him I looked straight down into his cockpit as he glanced back and up. For a split second, before he realised I wasn't a German that he'd allowed to get behind him and despite his goggles, I saw on Mitch's face a look of such pure open mouthed terror that I've never forgotten it.

I lost control of my machine as a result of my

instinctive kick on the rudder and was pleased to have to dive away to recover from the spin I fell into. As I climbed again and searched the sky above my upper wing for our bombing formation, I felt this second experience to be a kind of revelation, which didn't take my fear away but reassured me that others felt it too and therefore that it might be lived with.

Four

The Nines bombed Rozieres. I stared down, too fascinated not to despite my anxiety at what might be above us. Small dark billows would suddenly obscure the silver criss-cross of rails as the Nines' bombs exploded. A red roof I'd spotted was no longer there after the cloud that formed over it had dispersed.

Five of us accompanied the Nines back across the lines and then patrolled uneventfully among the clouds for another fifty minutes. Leigh hadn't rejoined us. He was shot, burnt, down on the other side a prisoner, gone home early with a dead engine or just plain lost. Mitch flew at fifteen thousand feet in wide semi-circles so that we could check our tails more easily. I determinedly studied each quarter of the sky in turn.

On all our flights, engine vibration conspired with the cold to remove all but the dullest feeling from the body. If you could smell in the cold, you smelt engine oil or cordite from the guns. Chewing gum soon became flavourless. You might still have the stale taste of breakfast egg in your mouth since anxiety seemed to stop digestion. The roar of the Wolseley Viper was louder than a pneumatic drill and sitting just behind it for two hours, despite helmet ear flaps, caused all of us to shout on landing when the sudden silence after the engine cut out rang continuously for ages. So those explosions I'd seen on the rails at Rozieres were sudden cueless eruptions and Mitch's Fokker had reared and tumbled soundlessly before us. In the air all your normal perceptions converged on the eyes. You hoped they'd spot Huns early enough to keep you alive or permit you to kill. The best killers had the best eyes.

After landing I can imagine how we clustered, raucous and excited, around Mitch and Shaw, the recording officer, at a table set outside the squadron office in the early morning sun of 7.30. We had to reduce that two hour maelstrom of aeroplanes and emotions to the few typed lines of an official combat report:

> *'B' Flight dived on a group of 8 enemy aircraft which were attacking the DH9s. Captain Mitchell of 'A' Flight fired at one which was seen to fall out of control by himself and 2nd Lieutenant Bridge. 2nd Lieut. Bridge and Lts. Baker and Butcher also fired at enemy aircraft inconclusively. 2nd Lt. Leigh did not return.*

Suddenly famished after a job and despite a headache, I would have demolished bacon and fried potatoes, tea and toast. Then as I remember, Mitch entered, back from telephoning Archie batteries for news of Leigh.

"No one saw anything! Goddamnit! I ought to take

better care of you guys. What had Leigh done? Two jobs? This bloody war!"

Perhaps Mitch felt too keenly the comparison with "Auntie" from the Camel squadron, who'd never lost anyone, and here, one of us had gone on our second flight.

"Don't feel too cut up, Mitch," Billy said, "there's no one any of us would sooner follow you know."

"It's a war, Mitch." Butcher said. "We've all got to take our chances." We all murmured assent but I for one was pleased to see him rise. "I'll just try Wing again. See if they've heard anything." I wanted him to worry. I wanted him to exert himself on our behalf, to bring us home alive.

I went for a bath then flopped in a deck chair in the sun outside the hut. I closed my eyes but what with 'C' Flight taking off and various engines running up and guns to the south-east there was no peace, so I went inside and lay down. My headache had dissipated to a knife above the eyebrows. I thought about what I should write to Constance but in my mind I could not decide how to start. "Dear Constance" sounded too conventional, "Darling" too intimate. Though we had been intimate, as newspapers used to say, I was not really sure of the grounds we'd been intimate on. If not exactly an amusement, I had perhaps satisfied a passing need. If I'd been offered love with no conditions, my native wit suggested caution since the face that came back to me from those few days at Billy's was that of Jessica, not Constance. Perhaps I shouldn't build conditions where none had been before.

So I turned over my greeting in my mind, "Dear", "Darling", "Dearest", or merely "Constance". I tried to replace Jessica's face with Constance's but failed, till memory moved from faces to the warm body Constance had offered me. Then the missing Leigh walked in. He had a limp, his uniform was torn, his face was muddy and his head was thrust through a British roundel painted on a piece of olive drab fabric from a wing.

"Bulls eye," he shrieked and twisted his face into a horrific leer. He crashed to the floor on his side and his face lost all colour and turned grey as his brain oozed from his ear onto the rug.

I sat up. The rug was clean. It was noon by my watch. I'd slept for two hours. My headache had gone, as headaches would at the beginning. Billy lay on his side on the bed across the room with his trench coat pulled over him, not quite snoring. I was glad of the sun falling through the window onto the rug. I wouldn't have liked to peer into darkness to see if Leigh really lay dead on my hut floor. Poor old Leigh, I thought and tiptoed out towards the sunshine. I'd already consigned Leigh to a grave I realised, and didn't care to grieve too long.

He'd been an entertaining chap though and knew countless verses to 'The Bold Aviator', which we'd sometimes raucously bawl out around a piano. He'd written some down for me which I have in front of me at this moment, the paper as brittle with age as I am now.

Take the piston rods out of my kidneys
And assemble the engine again.

They seem to me exactly the kind of nonsense we passed our time with when not flying or glancing through *Tatler, The Illustrated London News* or *La Vie Parisienne*. Of course, there was also the daily summary of air fighting from *The Times* of a week before to read. That was how we found out what we'd actually been up to. Often though, I'd just seek out three others who'd happily spend an hour or two at whist or bridge at a time thought inappropriate in civilian life.

'C' flight returned without Campbell and Hutton. No one had seen what happened to Campbell but Hutton was a flamer. Five miles over at ten thousand feet they were engaged with three Pfalz scouts when Fokker biplanes joined in. Hutton went straight down with his engine spewing flames which then engulfed the cockpit. The four survivors, including Thompson, the flight commander, looked pale. Three gone in a day and there were more jobs still to do. The major chivvied us all off for lunch. We'd just finished our corn beef when we heard a Wolseley. An SE circled the field and Campbell landed. He'd got lost and dropped in for directions twenty miles away at a French airfield where they'd given him an early lunch and practised their English.

That afternoon, I may have played tennis or lain in the sun or read, I'd brought *Howards End* in my valise, or perhaps I strolled around the perimeter of the field. That was how I passed my afternoons when there was another job in prospect. The guns continued from the south-east. The Aussies were attacking. We'd heard that much from Wing and our work that day and in the next few days was to support that attack. Later, after the war, as old combatants do, I read about what had happened and what battles I'd taken part in. Australians supporting a surprise tank attack had advanced six hundred yards on a two mile front on the Somme towards Morlancourt.

The weather was fine, the sunshine brilliant, although there was a threatening closeness in the air. It was a good day for lying in the sun, even if with a job to come at six it was impossible to relax.

We took off, formed up on Mitch to gain our height and then crossed the lines towards Sailly le Sec, passing Corbie, where Richthofen had been brought down in April. Clouds made life difficult for Archie and easier for us. We rose to sixteen thousand feet and Mitch led us through towering white canyons with sides like great walls of ice. Far below, the ground was grey and uninviting. The clouds were majestic and dazzling and might have made you believe in God but for the slaughter going on below and the thought that round the side of any cloud at any moment might come a dozen aeroplanes, each with two machine guns.

But of course, we were following Mitch. So as we rounded a billow of cumulo-nimbus we saw the five Albatros scouts two thousand feet below us that he later told us he'd been tracking. Mitch rocked his wings. We dived and the wires that braced my wings started a high-pitched singing above the engine's roar.

The Huns grew so rapidly before us that I feared we'd collide if they didn't move. I lined one up in my Aldis sight but then they saw us and split up. One dived away, foolish against SEs and a sure sign of wind up. Butcher and Billy on my left followed him down and I lost them against the grey of the earth as the others turned towards us.

A multi-coloured blur swept past me. I fired too late and kicked right rudder, feeling myself pushed down and sideways as the SE did a flat turn to follow him. I saw a yellow tail disappear like a ghost through the white wall of the bank of cloud now to my left. I pulled the stick into my stomach and retrieved the wing I'd also lost inside the cloud. I didn't like the sensation of disappearing into such a solid looking white mass. Though I'd have done it in the German pilot's situation, I didn't want moisture in my engine or a collision with an enemy I couldn't see. I found myself circling between the now threatening-looking grey-white clouds. All my colleagues and enemies had disappeared in those few seconds it had taken me to turn after the Albatros. I looked around me. I was cold meat alone. Mitch would have urged me to climb since height was safety. I forced myself to do that, though my instinct was to dive where I'd seen him lead. I flew back west, safe from Archie among the clouds, ready to dodge if a Hun appeared.

For all my care, I failed to see Baker's SE before it popped up alongside me. My heart was in my mouth, but instantaneously I recognised the machine and wanted to kiss it. I tucked in beside Baker and he led me back to the lines, where we patrolled honourably till our time was up.

That patrol was typical; a game of cat and mouse in which relaxation was impossible as you slowly froze. Then suddenly and often with no warning, you would have to react so violently that you became a shaking, heart-thumping wreck, unable for minutes afterwards to do more than fly in gentle circles. The machines that had caused the agitation would probably have gone as quickly as they'd appeared.

The others landed as we climbed out. We pulled off our flying suits in the ground-level warmth of the sun. The air was closer than ever and the clouds were thicker and greyer. From time to time a growl of thunder drowned the guns. The mechanics hurried to push the machines under cover.

"You should have shot him," Mitch was saying as we all joined up. "It's not enough to destroy machines, you've got to kill."

Butcher's Hun had got out with a parachute. Butcher and Billy had circled him and waved. The Hun had waved back.

"He was helpless," Billy protested.

"And he'll be back tomorrow," Mitch said. "What if he was the one got Leigh and Hutton? He'll get you tomorrow. It's not your bloody cricket, you know. This is a war and we've got to end up on top. Shoot the bastards."

"I know it's a war, Mitch," Butcher said, "but it's different when you see one of them hanging in the air, kicking his legs, waving his arms around. It's not like shooting at a machine. Christ, I'd like to see you do it! He was just a bloke like you and me."

"I'd do it," Mitch said, "I'd bloody well do it."

There was lightning. The first heavy drops of rain kicked dust up around us and we scurried in.

The argument of the parachute, the first anyone had seen, and the ethics of shooting at it continued in the mess as we stood at the windows and gazed out at the storm that crackled around the field. Most of us had succumbed to armchairs and drinks in the gloom the storm had caused when the door burst open and lightning flashed behind the dark figure that stood there. A flying suit was dumped on the floor and the man, wide-eyed and soaking, his tunic torn and his face muddy, stomped up to the bar, picked up the water jug and drank the contents off at one go as we gaped at him.

"Christ, I needed that," he said, "not a drink since dawn," and he put the jug back. Then he looked up and recognised our astonishment.

"What's up, you blokes? You look as if you've seen a ghost."

It was Leigh, back from the grave.

We immediately crowded around the lost sheep, all shouting questions at the same time. A delighted Mitch thrust a drink into Leigh's hand. I remember feeling momentarily put out that the dead man I'd already consigned to the past should have returned but thrust the thought from me in case it was a bad omen for my own fate.

A lifetime earlier, at dawn that day, Leigh had

suffered a series of the calamities we risked daily. Following Mitch in our dive on the Fokkers, Leigh's Vickers gun had jammed. He'd pulled out and away from the fight to check the cocking handle then gone through clearance procedure No. 2. This meant banging the breech with the small hammer we carried in a pocket at the side of the cockpit, hoping to clear a cartridge that may have been a thousandth of an inch too wide. Before he could succeed, he saw holes appear in the engine fairing ahead of him. He turned and dived and got away before the Hun pilot could lower his aim. He found himself very near the ground as he pulled out, fortunately with no one behind.

"The motor sounded dickey so I thought I'd better head for home and then just as I was passing a church I saw a flash from the roof and the engine cut out and down I went. Some blighter was up there with a machine gun."

"Didn't you switch to gravity?" Baker asked.

Confusion came over Leigh's smile-wreathed face.

"I didn't think of it," he confessed.

"Gosh," Billy said, "I wouldn't have either. I'd have been thinking where can I put down?"

"Always check your gravity," Baker said, "first thing."

"I expect poor old Leigh thought the engine had been shot up, what with the flash from the church roof and all." Billy said, sounding keen to rescue Leigh from the implied wind up.

"Well, I did, to be honest," Leigh said, grasping the lifeline. "And the next thing", he went on, "there was a terrible bang, and I was upside down in a shell-hole, trying to wriggle out and when I did, there were bullets flying across over my head and there was a rat about a yard away and we looked at each other and I swear we both thought, 'Put my head up? Not Pygmalion likely.' So I sat there with Ratty waiting for it to die down and after about a hundred years this Aussie popped his head over the rim and said, 'You all right, mate?' They'd just captured my shell-hole, so they pointed me away from the guns and went on their way. I started walking and here I am. Have I missed dinner?"

Leigh had committed serious errors, which were probably all fear induced, and through his naivety had been found out in them. When attacked, he dived and lost altitude, the key to air fighting. When his engine cut, he failed to switch to the gravity tank, a vain hope but his only one low down like that. Though he'd seen a gun flash, something else might have happened to his engine and the gravity tank might have given another ten minutes flying. There but for the grace of God, I thought, like at least one other there that night, as the rain pummelled the mess roof and we sat down to roast lamb, for I have that scene not from memory but from Billy's diary as he must have written it down very soon afterwards.

Dinner was spoilt that night, as it usually was, by a runner from wing who brought the next day's orders. The major would always open them, glance rapidly down as a silence fell over us, lay them aside and go on with his meal while making ostentatious conversation.

We would join in, perhaps too loudly. In his mind, he was deciding where and how he would send each of us into danger. I suppose too, that he wondered whose family he might have to compose a letter to in which he would avoid mentioning that we had burnt to a crisp while falling three miles to earth as poor Hutton had.

Mail might also arrive from wing during dinner and it was probably around this time that I received my first letter from Constance. I remember it well, since it solved the difficulty of how to address her. I was "Dear George", and amongst other things she wrote of the wonderful blackberry crop in prospect for 1918. If Constance and I were to discuss soft fruit in our letters, and there were wild strawberries that had somehow survived in the banks around the airfield, I did not feel too guilty that Jessica's was the face I remembered and not hers.

Later, as I lay motionless in the dark, the dangers of the next morning's job tormented me. We would take off at ten and patrol, but only after dropping bombs in support of the Australians on whatever we could find; trenches, machine guns, artillery. Eventually, after what seemed hours, I succeeded in driving those images away with thoughts of Jessica.

I remembered Jessica as I had seen her on that last day. Full of the memory of Constance's body though I was then, the sight of Jessica and of her long fingers as she stroked the face of Satan, her fierce looking black stallion, captivated me. She murmured words to him that were indistinguishable to me, though I was only a careful six feet away from them. She gazed unblinking into Satan's eyes and blew into his nostrils. Horse and owner seemed totally enthralled by each other. I wondered if Billy, who leant nonchalantly with his elbow on the top of the fence felt jealous. I would have. In fact I did. Then Jessica moved to Satan's side and with a quick hop, threw herself over his bare back and pulled herself up and astride. White knuckles gripped the mane and with a kick from Jessica's heels, Satan wheeled away from us and quickly broke into a gallop towards the huge oak at the far end of the field.

The sun fell full on them both and Satan's black coat shone. Jessica sat still and upright on the horse's back and her hair streamed out above her white blouse. I saw Billy gazing after her as she moved into the distance. Beyond her were more fields, some turning golden, hedges, trees and eventually the sea, with a line of puffy white clouds above the horizon. Billy and I lounged in the shade at the edge of the paddock.

Suddenly, Satan wheeled and galloped back. Then, thirty yards off, he wheeled again and galloped across in front of us and Jessica disappeared.

"It's all right," Billy said as I must have cried out. "Look!" Jessica's head had appeared in front of Satan's neck. She rode like that for another fifty yards half-hidden from our sight. She was hanging over Satan's side with her legs holding her on his back and her arms wrapped tight around his neck. I didn't see anyone ride this way again until in Hollywood ten years later I watched Indians reproduce this bareback trick for celluloid.

"She's showing off," Billy said. "I do apologise. But she is a frightfully good rider."

Jessica pulled herself upright again and turned Satan to gallop straight towards us. The sound of pounding hooves grew. I was about to vault the fence when Satan stopped, it seemed in a yard, raising dust from the dry earth at the trampled edge of the field. Jessica slid from his back in one movement but kept her arm round his neck as Satan bent his head and nuzzled her breast. She murmured and stroked his face again and he snorted. These two were lovers I thought as I drifted into sleep that night in my airfield hut in France, and Billy and I were voyeurs.

In the morning we hared after Mitch across the lines at tree top height. The clouds were at two thousand feet and the altitude we could have gained would only have made a better target of us. As it was, we were past before gunners could draw a bead. The Australian attack was forcing the Germans to move in daylight and we caught a column of artillery on an open road. We had to rise to two hundred feet so that the bombs would arm themselves on their way down. Mitch led the way and bombed first. Silent clouds of dust appeared above the road, guns tumbled and fell askew, terrified horses ran harnessed together dragging a shattered limber, men in grey scattered in all directions. I dropped my four twenty-five pound bombs too but I didn't aim very carefully. I glanced behind constantly, telling myself I would not be surprised by Hun scouts but actually not wanting to watch the carnage too closely. We turned and flew back to machine gun the horrific scene. Bullets kicked up spurts of dust and chased men and horses up the road.

I was sickened but duty meant I couldn't pull up and fly away. One horse lay writhing by a ditch, still harnessed to a gun. That morning, it was really only that horse that I took aim at. I saw it collapse and lie still before I zoomed up after Mitch.

We fled back across the lines since Mitch had said he wouldn't patrol beneath the overcast. As we crossed, I noticed Leigh, flying the squadron's spare machine, begin to descend, slowly at first, and then faster. I dived under Mitch and waggled my wings and pointed. We banked and watched Leigh fall into a slow spin, turn twice and hit the ground near the ruins of Villers-Bretonneux. There was no hope for him. Back from the grave yesterday he'd been hit from the ground today and was probably unconscious or already dead before he went in.

He was one of only four squadron casualties to fall on our side of the lines. This was the result of RAF policy laid down by Trenchard and dating from RFC days early in the war: always attack. Then, it was even considered un-British to take evasive action when fired at by an enemy aircraft. This and other absurdities like the non-adoption of parachutes because pilots might abandon their aircraft prematurely were the decisions of those on high to be carried out by us below.

Years afterwards I read of all this as I tried to make

sense of what I'd lived through. It was even suggested in what I read that the German policy of patrolling only over their own territory was a better use than ours of scarce resources of men and machines. But I also read of the panic and chaos caused by our low level bombing and strafing during attacks. The German offensive of March 1918, I read, would never have been stopped but for the round the clock disruption of the enemy's troop movements by our low flying aircraft.

In the days following Leigh's death, there was more of the same. Our principal task was to protect the real low fliers, Sopwith Camels, from interference by Hun patrols but we always started with a few bombs to drop in Hunland. Then we would climb to whatever height we could reach in the almost continuous bad weather, which never seemed to get so bad that we couldn't fly. We would buzz around just below the clouds at five thousand feet, watching for Huns and constantly dodging Archie, for whom we were a wonderful target etched against the overcast.

One day the weather improved and we escorted bombers to Bray railway station. Mitch and Baker got Fokkers in another diving chase. The next day there was constant wind and rain. We were sent over when a break appeared but landed soaked, the rain pounding on the fabric of our wings after we'd cut our engines. Hill, Leigh's replacement, taken across because there'd be no Huns around, turned over on landing. He cracked his head and was sent off to hospital.

Johnson my fitter went down with influenza. I

walked over to see him on the duck boards that had been laid in this unseasonal weather between our quarters and the messes. He looked awful and said little. There was an epidemic. Thirty men at 74 Squadron had died, though no officers I believe. My mother wrote. Influenza was an epidemic at home, too. Some of the shops were closed because of it. Mrs Mason, three doors up was very bad. Mr Webster, a special constable had died of it. I should be careful not to get it myself.

But I had bigger worries. The next day I nearly died. We ran into some Fokker pilots who knew what they were about. It's in my log book.

25th July, 5.30 – 8.00 pm. Offensive patrol between Morlancourt and Bapaume. Height 18,000 feet. Capt. Mitchell, Lts. Baker and Butcher, 2nd Lts. Love and Bridge. Long engagement with Fokker biplane. Hits observed. Landed on gravity tank.

What a masterpiece of condensed summary! My mouth went dry for years at the memory.

"They came down at us. Mitch saw them and showed them to us but they were above and came down before we could get on top. Visibility was good. Behind us was the curve of the sea and you could almost imagine England through the final haze. The sun glinted on their wings as they banked to dive and then the world accelerated.

"A turn and climb to face them. Then at once the quick kaleidoscope of earth and sky, below, above, to right, to left, and diving, climbing, turning biplanes, coloured tails, black crosses outlined with white, red streamers from an SE's struts. Heavy in the turn, forced into the seat, even your arm a weight. Peer through the Aldis sight. A black cross fills it. Fire! It's gone. Too slow. Stick over. Sky left, earth right. In front, no Hun. To right, no Hun. To left, above, below, no Huns. Screw neck right round. Clear sky beyond the tail. Strain neck the other side. To the right the earth is miles away. Back harder with the neck. It's there! Oh, God, it's there! A red tail. Curving in behind, at right angles to the earth, like me. Shrink in the cockpit, shrink inside the flying suit, make yourself smaller! Shrink! Stick back! Stick back! Don't dive! He's far too close. Never dive. 'Turn! Keep turning!' Mitch says. A metronome. 'Keep turning!'

"Red tail turning, too. Turn tighter. Throttle back. Engine note changes. Stick back. Stick back. How many turns? Ten? Never mind. Don't count. Stick back. Turn on forever. But you can't. The wind. Taking you east. East into Hunland. Only his red tail in vision now. When that's gone, he'll be right behind and you'll be dead. Cold meat. What to do? Mitch, what to do? He's gone from sight. He's right behind. Stick over. Half roll. Pull out. Sky above again. Neck round, neck round! He's there! Kick rudder left. Skid left. Look back. Still there. Twenty yards behind! Full throttle! Stick forward. Dive. Stick back. A zoom. But not with a Fokker behind. Kick left, stick left. Earth to the left, sky to the right. Flick, flick, flick. Holes in the wing to the right. Your head was there.

"The ground much closer to the left now. Head round. He's there! Red tail. He'll disappear again and you'll be dead. He's good. Too good for you. Where's Mitch? Half roll again, pull out, skid left. Flick, flick, in the canvas of the wing. Half roll, pull out, reverse direction, turn, stick back. Screw back your eyes to see. Your neck! That screaming pain! He's there! Still there!

"Where's west? Which way is home? You're going down. Each half roll takes you lower. Keep your eyes back, watch him! He'll show you when to turn or skid. Gun flashes. Flick, flick, flick behind. The sun! On the horizon! West! That's home!

"Surprise the Hun! Do something new! Roll upside down. The earth above. Stick back and when the earth's in front, stick central, open throttle. Dive and dive! And watch the lovely earth come up. 180 now. The Fokker can't keep up. Or can he? No. They zoom, don't dive. Stick back, but gently, gently, breaking nothing. Two hands now. Pull back. The ground is close. And everything is large. It's very close. Stick right back now. You weigh a ton. The horizon floats up in front and the weight slips off you. Now the sky sits high above. Strain round to search for red tail. No. The other side? No red tail there. Thank God! But don't fly straight! Bank left, bank right but keep on west. Brown bears appearing left and right. Wumpf! Wumpf! Oh, hallo Archie. Pleased to see us? Look back. Nothing.

"Back across the lines you're weak, your grip gone as if you just woke up. Can't think, can't move, can't fly except to fly on straight and level. Ten minutes till you can honourably go home. Where are the others? No idea. All dead? The world slows down again.

"When I landed, I couldn't push myself up on the cockpit rim to climb out. A mechanic put his hands under each armpit and lugged me out. I sat on the wing and pulled off my helmet, utterly exhausted and weak from relaxed tension. The mechanic counted sixty seven bullet holes in my tailplane, fuselage and lower starboard wing.

"'Jeez!' Mitch said. 'I saw you going round with that Fokker but I knew you'd be OK. Did you get him?'"

Billy nearly died that day too and that is the description he wrote in his diary that evening, 25th July. We were all shaken but I'd put bullets into the Hun I was turning with. Mitch's had flopped into a spin and then disappeared. We had all come home. It counted as a victory. We hung up our flying gear and collapsed on our beds, ears ringing, heads aching, necks stiff, limbs trembling from engine vibration and sudden released tension. As they usually were, our minds were crammed full of a whirling mass of tumbling aeroplanes and clouds, with sky and earth at peculiar angles, which Billy later exorcised, or tried to, by writing it down.

The weather turned bad for flying. There was heavy overcast, low clouds and rain, drizzle and ground mist that we couldn't get up through. It was wonderful weather, which should have been good for pilots. But always there was the chance of a break when the sun would dry windows and make it possible to get off and patrol the clouds. Then we would become knights galloping around great white and grey battlemented fortresses and towers. Or wing would telephone that Archie had spotted Huns and we should chase them home whatever the conditions.

So despite the awful weather, there was no chance of relaxation, and not a single carefree day of leisure. We sat around and yarned or played at whist or bridge or stared lasciviously at the girls in Kirchner prints. We played the gramophone, too, while gazing listlessly at showers blown slanting and grey across the field, waiting for a telephone call or a shaft of sunshine from the heavens. The days were colourless, damp and depressing. Though just nineteen, I sometimes felt that I was moving slowly down a grim tunnel, whose roof I held up with my shoulders, towards a far distant point of daylight that signalled safety. The weight of rock above at any moment though might prove too great and bury me; shut off the longed for daylight.

As I write this, my shoulders are again weighed down and my few remaining days pass in much the same way as then, though the tunnel has become a cave since no far distant light now beckons. I wait expectantly for the stroke or heart attack that has taken the place a bullet from a Spandau once held in my mind. I likewise dread incontinence, paralysis, senility in the way I once dreaded fire in the air or collapsing wings that might have sent me plummeting to earth with minutes full of seconds to review my life and contemplate eternity.

Glover was shot down from the ground and killed. Baker was shot up so badly that both wheels were punctured by bullets and he crashed on landing. Oughton of 'B' Flight was a flamer. Butcher got flu and retired to bed all smiles. We went en masse to entertain him till he threw us out. The major organised a rag. We drank too much and bruised ourselves on furniture and other people's knees at rugby in the mess. Baker was a flamer. Billy and I watched him go. Mitch, a psychologist, took us up contour chasing in the afternoon to raise our spirits but afterwards, while checking rounds outside the armourer's hut in rare early evening sun, Billy and I relived the experience.

On the morning patrol at fifteen thousand feet, we'd caught a Hun two-seater going home from a photo-reconnaissance. The sun was there from time to time between the clouds. As we swung in anticipation round each gigantic ball of cumulus, it was a little like turning cards over in Pelmanism but more throat-catching since a Hun patrol was the possible surprise. Suddenly Mitch turned east and climbed. I searched the sky but to no avail. Minutes later, we swung west again and, diving out of the sun, banked around a huge curve of gleaming cloud which had hidden the DFW Mitch had spotted.

The Hun pilot put his nose down, since it was a fast machine, but we were faster in our dive. Mitch slipped below to fire from the Hun crew's blind spot while Baker engaged the observer from above. It was too crowded around the two-seater to get a shot, so I throttled back to watch. The pilot's head fell and the DFW slid to the right. The observer continued to return Baker's fire until the guns suddenly went vertical and the German disappeared, obviously hit. The Hun turned on its back and the nose slowly went down. Something dark fell from it and I watched in horror as the object grew limbs which flailed as it fell. I was grateful for the appalling noise of the engine, which covered any screams I might otherwise have heard. As I banked away and my lower wings hid the falling man and his aeroplane, I saw a blue tongue lick along the side of Baker's engine, then suddenly envelop the whole front of the machine in a sheet of orange flame that the slip stream swept back into the cockpit.

Alone in our tiny machines three miles above the earth, though we were only yards away, we were powerless to help Baker. He must have put the stick over or perhaps it was an instinctive reaction as he tried to escape from the flames because his SE dived straight for a grey-tinged cloud that might have borne rain. It swallowed him but for a second or two glowed spectrally from within before it became opaquely grey again. We spiralled down around the cloud. Before we reached its base two thousand feet below, we could see that the breeze was already dispersing the smudgy plume of black that the burning SE still trailed towards the ground.

That spectral glow from within the cloud sat in my mind as Billy and I silently checked .303 cartridges with a gauge, making a large pile between us. Mitch was keen to avoid stoppages in the air since when they happened, we were vulnerable and useless. He encouraged us to check ammunition ourselves as an example to the armourers. Behind us on a board above the door to the armourer's hut was an admonition to the men:

"A man's life depends on your work. Don't cut corners."

Suddenly, Billy asked, "How fast do you accelerate as you fall, George?"

I knew the answer.

"32 feet per second. Every second 32 feet a second faster, so after ten seconds your speed is 320 feet per second."

Billy imbibed this fact in silence and we continued with our gauges.

In the hut before dinner, while I persevered with *Howards End* again, Billy busied himself with pen and paper. Another letter to Jessica I thought until he came up and showed me the columns of figures on the page in the diary which I have before me now.

"Look George, you're the brains in this hut, have I got this right?"

He'd calculated speeds of fall and timings.

"We were at fifteen thousand feet, so that Hun must have taken thirty seconds to hit the ground."

He had added 32 to 32, then 32 to 64 then 32 to 96, 30 times. The total came to 14,890 feet – our altitude more or less.

"And look, is this right? His speed at 30 seconds – 960 feet per second, times 60 for minutes, times 60 for an hour, comes to 3,456,000 feet, divided by 5,280 feet in a mile, comes to 654 miles per hour. That's what they were doing when they hit the ground. 654 mph. You'd make a fair-sized hole, wouldn't you?"

I stared at the horrifying page and its logic horrifies me still.

"The calculations look right," I said, "but I doubt if they reached that speed or that their fall was as quick as that because of air resistance." I dredged up Physics matriculation. "They would have reached terminal velocity sometime before they hit the ground."

Billy stared at me as I explained how, when weight and air resistance are in equilibrium, the falling body can no longer accelerate and it falls at a constant speed: terminal velocity.

"It depends on the size of the object and the shape," I said, "something streamlined would go faster. Waving his arms and legs around like that would have slowed the Hun up but if he'd tucked his arms in and gone head first, he'd have built up speed."

"Faster that a burning SE?"

"I should think so"

"So if Baker had taken a dive over the side head first, he'd have hit quicker."

"Probably. But not nearly as quick as thirty seconds."

"How long?"

"God knows. Two or three minutes. Five? I don't know really."

Billy shuddered.

"Imagine what that's like, George. Like one of those awful dreams. Poor old Baker! I hope he had his pistol and blew his brains out then as he always said he would."

Soon after that Mitch started his master classes. One damp afternoon, teacup in hand, Billy said.

"How do you do it, Mitch? I shoot at Huns all the time but none of them go down."

"You're not close enough. If you're close enough, you can't miss."

"How close?"

"Fifty yards? Twenty yards?'

"Twenty yards? But how do you get that close?"

Then Mitch got a tennis ball to imitate the sun and with our hands spread out in front of us as pretend aeroplanes, we stood on chairs to climb into the sun and dived on Mitch's spread out hands when he commanded us, making a mock air fight in the mess.

"If the Hun's above you when you spot him, turn away and climb and come back in the sun. Only fight if you're above."

He took to asking sudden questions when walking back across the field, when playing tennis, over tea.

"You're coming home at zero feet, ten miles to go and bullets smash your windscreen. What do you do?" or "You're on your gravity tank at five thousand feet on the other side and you see a Fokker dropping on your tail. What do you do?

"If you think about these things before they happen," he explained, "you might just get back home alive."

It was about this time that the RAF's great killer, Mannock, went down, shot from the ground. The story spread through the squadrons. He was a classic leader, caring for his men, anxious to kill and bring all his followers home. Mitch was affected. He had known the great man and had made Mannock's ideas on how to fight his own: always from above, seldom from the same level, never from below. Mannock had had these slogans painted on a hangar wall, Mitch said. He became even more anxious to kill and took to glaring at the clouds and rain through the dripping windows of the mess.

Five

The Germans still wanted Amiens. After dark, guns were a constant rumble and mutter below all other sounds and just before dawn, if we were unlucky enough to be awake, the horizon to the south-east was lit with orange flashes. There was a sinister beauty there that I missed in later years as I missed the comradeship of those young men I was thrown in among. Mitch was twenty-three and seemed absurdly mature and wise. The major was twenty-five and like a grandfather. He was already a captain in 1916 when he transferred from his regiment and became a second-lieutenant again for the flying. But many of us, like Billy and I, were just out of school, nineteen or twenty, innocent of the world but growing up quickly and becoming less certain by the day of all those things we had once been sure of.

One day we flew two patrols, the first uneventful, the second an evening tour of gleaming, bulging cloud walls as Mitch led us in feint and counter feint against patrols of Fokkers and Albatroses. Eventually we fell in a dive on a two-seater that made me scream at the pain in my ears. The German burst into flames and tumbled down, smudging the brilliant clouds as it went. I was pleased to go home but I was so agitated still from that dive that I had to circle the field twice before I felt calm enough to land safely.

The evening was fine. Released from flying, we attempted tennis on the wet grass and then walked to the village in the late sun. Billy threw sticks for the black and white mongrel that accompanied us, one of the many strays that always seemed to congregate around airfields and airmen. Billy loped along behind the dog, rather like a hound himself. We laughed on our way at the dog's enjoyment of the game and forgot our work for a while. In the village estaminet, we drank pale French beer and spoke to gunner subalterns.

"The Hun's finished, isn't he, George?" Billy said. "When we come across them, they just turn for home. We have to shoot them to put them out of their misery."

One of the gunners played the piano. We sang 'Tipperary', 'Keep the home fires burning' and felt like real soldiers, although the songs that the real soldiers sang were, like their language, totally obscene. Officers from the Bristol Fighter squadron which shared our field watched us with silent smiles. The gunners left and Billy sat down to play but before his fingers could touch the keys one of the Bristol men, a captain, had crossed the room and lowered the lid gently.

"Pilots don't play this," he said.

Billy turned on the stool. "Why ever not?"

"They just don't. Not now. The last four who did are dead."

"Good God. What rot, eh, George?" But as Billy looked up at me, the confidence and excitement had fled from his eyes. He left the lid closed and we walked home as the very last of the light went and pale flashes began to illuminate the skyline to the south-east.

Mitch warned us for an early job, an airfield raid with the Bristol Fighter squadron. The major would lead but Mitch devised the plan. We listened silently as he spent half an hour laying it out to us; an obvious procedure though later I realised it was something not all flight commanders did.

Remembering the piano, I lay in bed pondering superstition. My mother threw salt over her shoulder, uncrossed knives, forbade new shoes to be placed on a table. Flyers were notorious for superstition. Carrying good luck charms, touching the rudder, putting the same glove on first; I did all those things. I flew with a St. Christopher medallion in my tunic pocket. I'd put it there when it arrived from my mother just before my first solo, when I succeeded in handling the Avro's Clerget rotary engine properly and managed to put her down in just the right place. With something as uncertain as flying in the aeroplanes of 1918, it was often difficult to know what it was we'd done which had ensured our survival and so we tended to repeat the process religiously, frightened to vary it according to logic.

I woke in the dark and immediately remembered the airfield raid. I felt cold despite my blankets.

Across the room a cigarette glowed. I saw myself over the Hun airfield, my SE at the centre of tracers coming up from all sides seeking the cockpit and my vulnerable flesh. I heard machine guns behind me and kicked the rudder, but too late, blood oozed from my Sidcot suit, flowed from my lips as I coughed. The SE ploughed into the ground and exploded in a rolling ball of flame.

I sat up and felt for my cigarettes. The match blinded me. Billy must have seen my pale face in the flare. He spoke slowly and sounded glum.

"Sometimes I feel I won't come back from all this, you know. I wish I was like you, George, always calm."

"Me!" I said, astonished.

"Yes. Nothing ever ruffles you."

I laughed.

"You see. I wish I could laugh. I'm lying here in a blue funk, smoking, because if I try to sleep, I keep seeing Fokkers chasing me down like the other day or machine guns hitting me over that damned Hun aerodrome. Oh God, for some more rain!"

"Amen to that," I said.

Billy had surprised me but I was pleased to hear his confession. I added mine.

"But I'm not sure if I can get in that machine tomorrow," Billy protested.

"Nor am I," the darkness gave me courage to say.

"I've never been so frightened in my life," Billy said as if to explain himself before going on.

"And you're so alone up there. No one can help. In a regiment you'd have the men and the other officers near you but up there, if someone gets behind you, it's up to you. I'm not sure if I can cope. I don't feel in command of things, least of all myself." He paused. "I nearly wet myself the other day."

I laughed in recognition.

"I thought it was just me."

"Do you feel the same?"

"Yes."

"Honestly?"

"Oh, yes," I said. "But I'd feel worse if I let Mitch down. And if we refused to fly, they'd tear our wings off and send us home. It might be worse than death."

"If it was a quick death," Billy said. "But what about Baker and that Hun flamer the other day? Fancy going down like that, falling and falling, burning."

He made a shuddering noise in the dark. He stubbed out his cigarette and his voice came from nowhere.

"If they tore my wings off, I'd never be able to go home. I'd never be able to face Pa. Or Jessica."

"We have to do it," I said. "We did it today. It's just the waiting I suppose. We've got more chance with Mitch than with anybody. If he can't get us home, no one can."

A match flared and I saw Billy's face lit in relief like a stone carving.

"Mitch is wonderful," he said. "In daylight I feel I could follow him anywhere. But at night, God! All the goblins come out."

"Mitch will watch us," I said. "And we can watch each other, too, check each other's tail."

"I suppose so. How long till dawn?"

I struck a match. My watch showed 1.45.

"Two hours."

"Oh, God!" He put out his cigarette and I heard bedclothes and springs as he slid down.

This became the pattern of our nights when there were early jobs. We'd lie awake plagued by fears, bolster each other up and renew our faith in Mitch before going back separately to machine guns and Fokkers and eventually to sleep, which I must have done that night for immediately my shoulder was shaken and a voice said,

"3.45, sir. Clear skies"

I am sure we made our way as usual with nervous banter through the damp dawn air towards our dark machines, as still as paper cut outs against the lightening eastern sky. No whale grease that day since we would not go above two thousand feet. I kicked my way through dewy grass and braced myself for what was to come. Though I occupied myself with routine, my stomach was not deceived. I walked around the SE and checked the rudder, elevators and ailerons. I climbed up and slid down from the fuselage top into my cane seat, strapped in, reached up for the Lewis gun, counted spare magazines, tore open chewing gum and finally checked the revolver I'd been carrying since Baker's long burning fall. Then I pulled on gauntlets and started the engine with the stick right back to keep the tail on the ground. The machine and I shook and trembled, waiting for Mitch's Very light to flare up and arc through the gloom, the signal to taxi out.

We took off and rendezvoused over the field. The engine roar covered all other sound as the Bristol Fighters moved silently in beside us at two thousand feet. They were very safe machines and just as splitarse as SE5s. The pilot did the fighting with his Vickers gun but behind him, guarding his tail from diving Fokkers with a Lewis gun on a rotating Scarff ring was an observer. One of them waved to me as I looked across enviously at his pilot, who could safely concentrate on the view ahead. For him a tap on the shoulder rather than bullets through the windscreen would be the announcement of Huns behind.

We crossed the lines near Albert and immediately dived, for Mitch's plan was a low level dash into Hunland and then a turn back to appear over the airfield unannounced from the east. 'C' Flight kept watch above at ten thousand feet and another squadron's dawn patrol gave more protection at twenty thousand feet. Treetops, roofs, ruins, church towers sped past just below and to the side. The hundred pounds of bombs that hung inches beneath my feet made this a less than exhilarating experience. So low and with the extra weight, the SE felt much slower to respond to the controls. A lucky bullet or an engine cut out would have sent me, bombs and all, into whatever was ahead with no chance to avoid it. The air was bumpy and the machine would fall without warning and then slowly claw its way back up, the engine snarling as I pulled on the stick. Despite the hundred mile an hour wind past the windscreen, I was hot and my jaw ached from chewing. We leaped a river, caused a horse pulling a cart to bolt through a meadow, and suddenly the Hun airfield was dead ahead. Mitch banked left and we fell into line astern heading for hangars and the black crossed machines ranged in front of them.

Many years later in the Charing Cross Road, I came upon the translated memoirs of a German pilot, Erhard Moesle, and in one chapter recognised our raid. I prefer Moesle's view to the more impersonal version in Jones's *The War in the Air*, classic though that book is. Moesle says:

The English came at us over the trees, out of the dawn. We heard their engines and knew what was coming before we saw them. I ran from my machine to one of the guns set up near the hangars.

I remember the long shadows cast by the men who detached themselves from the machines they were preparing for take off in the very first light of the sun, which for them was only just appearing over the horizon. Most of them fled to the obvious protection of nearby hangars but two enemy machines moved out of the line, their pilots more ready for take off or more foolhardy than the others. As planned, Mitch and Butcher banked away from us to follow them. Moesle saw this too:

Ferdy and Wolfie had already started up and tore across the grass but the Tommies caught them just as they got into the air. It was madness for them to have tried. They crashed and burnt in the middle of the field.

A lifetime on I can now only imagine how my machine leaped when I released the bombs as I flew over a hangar, and how the black crossed machines ranged outside the hangars swelled in size; how I looked behind on each side for diving Huns, because I always did, but saw only the flight of Bristol Fighters following on.

Moesle had a different experience:

Bombs started falling and debris flew everywhere as explosions rent the air, drowning the roar of aero engines as the Tommies flew down our line of Fokkers, machine gunning them to matchwood. My gun was soon hot and the Tommies looked easy to hit to a pilot used to a twisting, turning target but I didn't get a single one.

I was always grateful to find that at times like that activity would flush fear away temporarily. Our targets here didn't move, so I had a chance to hit them, but I wasn't skilful enough to do that easily. I had to hunch down in the cockpit, lean forward and stare through the Aldis sight, nudge the rudder bar and control column until the target ahead filled the sight, then touch the gun trigger on the control stick to make dust kick up around the enemy machine ahead. A Vickers gun belt held only four hundred rounds. You could shoot the whole lot off without realising, so you counted. One thousand, two thousand, three thousand, then thumb off and back with the stick a fraction and on to the next machine. There must have been half a dozen of these unattended targets, one after the other, with not a human being visible.

Then, as the SE rose again and there were no more machines and the boundary road appeared, I can still imagine as I pulled the stick back and the machine zoomed, how my concentration would have fled and my fear would have returned. I would instantly have banked into a climbing turn, deciding anxiously whether or not the engine had the correct straining note to its deafening roar in this attitude. To my left would have been the watery blue early morning sky and to my right the cindered apron area in front of the German hangars and then the grass field beyond them. A reverse bank would have put the earth to my left and the sky to my right as I endeavoured to throw off the aim of any hidden German machine gunner below. I would have seen the line of aeroplanes we had machine-gunned seemingly untouched apart from one that was burning, and the Bristol Fighters that had followed us down, unloading bombs on the already blazing hangars.

Moesle says;

The air above was buzzing with aeroplanes bombing and strafing. Suddenly one of the English in a single-seater flew straight at my hangar, shooting into it. I fired off a whole belt at him but he swept over me and was gone.

Here my memory is sure. A Bristol Fighter crossed ahead of me and in panic, suddenly bereft of flying skill, I pulled the nose up with my speed too low and felt the SE wallow and my stomach drop as we shed flying speed and moved towards a stall. I had to bank left into a dive, the only answer even so close to the ground, then had to pull the stick back as it seemed I must bury the machine into the ground. I found myself speeding towards an open canvas hangar as yet untouched. Inside it, an Albatros scout rested on rigging trestles. White faces stared at me from the ground. I touched the trigger. There was nothing else I could do. It was my job. I hoped my spray of bullets would pass over the men but might hit the machine. A zoom carried me above the hangar roof and I climbed away to catch my breath. I had not spotted Moesle but I would have quartered the sky, searching for the flash of sun on diving wings, kicking the rudder every few seconds to skid away from invisible Huns with swivelling machine guns.

Moesle goes on:

Ammunition was exploding in the hangar to my left. A column of black smoke rose from it towards the heavens. I abandoned my gun and moved away from the explosions. The Tommies circled, looking for more targets. Then one of them, flying low, put his nose down and glided in on the far side of the field half a kilometre away. One of us had hit someone.

"Look!" cried my sergeant, "let's get him." But the Tommies still circled. I put a restraining hand on the sergeant's shoulder. We saw the pilot climb out, walk a few feet away and fire a flare at his machine. It brewed up instantly.

"I do not envy him his situation," I thought and decided to be in at his capture to protect him from the likes of my sergeant. Then, "Look!" I cried, amazed, as another English single-seater flew in low towards the burning wreck, landed and swung around it without stopping. The pilot I had pitied ran to his comrade's wing and was carried aloft. Again I did not envy him his situation standing on a wing, clutching on to the struts in a hundred mile an hour gale but I envied him

his gallant friend and stopped the sergeant shooting at them with his carbine as they flew away west with their friends swooping in to cluster round them. As the sound of our visitors died away, I heard the crackle of flames and the cries and shouts of the wounded and I could run to Ferdy and Wolfie. We lost twenty nine men including four pilots that morning and only two machines remained serviceable from sixteen. The English had put one over on us. But still today I would like to shake the hand of the pilot who rescued his friend.

We flew back low, anxious all the way, but our recent advances had moved the front line nearer and we buzzed across quite soon though we had to fly on to find a field that was safe for Mitch to put his passenger down in. Smart and I circled overhead. I was cock-a-hoop and felt like stunting but was too nervous after combat to do so. Billy slid from Mitch's wing and lay flat out on the ground for a moment but then stood up and waved to us.

Mitch's action had been inspiringly courageous and it bound us all even more under his spell. Billy, particularly, was bewitched. When he arrived back that day though, just after lunch, having walked and hitched lifts from the field where Mitch had left him, and as he told everyone the story again and again, secretly the thought crept in and grew in my mind as time went by that in Billy's position I would not have been quite so ecstatic about my rescue from imprisonment.

After the initial fear and worry of capture, having been brought down safely and honourably while doing his duty, Billy might have enjoyed a comfortable retirement from fighting. He wouldn't have been missed. The Yanks were arriving in France in good numbers and we couldn't really lose the war. In Billy's shoes I might have been put out that my interfering flight commander had rescued me so that I could place myself in danger again.

Instead, Billy stood drinks and sang songs with his arm round Mitch's shoulder and challenged the Camel squadron to a football match the next day. The major, who had witnessed it all, put in a recommendation for a VC for Mitch and this day or the next, Johnson, my fitter, who had thought war flying too dangerous an occupation to contemplate, died of influenza.

I stared for an hour at a blank sheet of paper, trying to think of words that might mean something to his widow, Dolly. Not for the first time my officer status was forcing me into an adulthood that at nineteen years of age I didn't really feel I'd attained. Eventually I must have strung together sufficient banalities and platitudes that I could sign my name below them and go off on another of those patrols which we seemed to undertake day after day. In between showers and squalls, we would take off and climb through the weather to where we could bank around huge mountains of cloud, quite brilliantly white in the sunshine. At any moment I might have to dive ten thousand feet or pull the stick back into my stomach to face an attack, engine snarling at full throttle, adrenalin flowing, so that ten minutes later I would be the usual trembling wreck fit only to fly in gentle circles.

But there were small escapes to be had. To the north of the field the land rose a little and when among the trees, you really could imagine yourself in Kent. Billy and I walked there on the day that he crashed while taking off.

It was my day off and as Mitch taxied 'A' flight out at 9 a.m. I was on my way to the mess to look for someone to drive to Amiens with. Two hundred feet up, Billy's engine cut. His reaction was text book. Despite the attractive empty field behind him, a turn towards which would have caused a sudden drop in airspeed, a stall and loss of control, he put the nose down and ploughed straight on at eighty miles an hour. The bank of the sunken road beyond the field ripped off the undercarriage. A tree on the bank tore away the port wings and the SE swung and slid on its belly, four bombs and all, across the sodden wheat field on the other side.

I waited for the explosion and a ball of flame as I bounced in the back of the tender across the field towards the wreck but it never came. I scrambled up the bank. Billy was sitting on a fallen tree trunk by the hedge fifty yards from the wreckage, still in helmet, goggles and leather face mask. As I ran over, he pulled them off and dropped them at his feet. He buried his white face in his hands.

I skirted the wreck and squatted down beside him.

"I crashed my bus, George," he said. "The major will be peed off."

He was shaking as we walked him away and he

stumbled on the deep rutted earth at the side of the field.

The major though said "stout effort" and washed him out for the rest of the day. I helped Billy to his bed and piled my blankets on top of his as he lay shivering despite the August warmth. His face was ashen, his eyes closed and his teeth clamped together to stop them chattering. I took his hand to slide it under the blankets and it gripped mine tight and would not let it go. I stayed there, as I might have to reassure a sick child, until after ten minutes or so, his grip relaxed and he fell asleep, allowing me to creep away. Sleep was still a great restorative then. He emerged for lunch, pale no more, and dragged me off towards the trees, keen to enjoy his unexpected holiday. Letters had just arrived from Jessica and he talked of her.

This wood reminded him of woods he'd wandered in with her at home; his father's woods. The woods I offered in exchange were far less grand, at Bellingham and Bromley, woods I'd ventured to on bikes with friends from Lewisham. The first tree he'd climbed was an oak that had grown for five hundred years beyond the ha-ha. Mine was by the West Kent Grammar School on Hilly Fields at Ladywell, one of the oases in the desert of London, which to my great surprise forty or fifty years on, I recognised in Henry Williamson's novels of the Great War.

While I had trekked from park to recreation ground, Jessica and Billy had grown up unfettered in the countryside, though Billy of course was actually unfettered only in the holidays from Eton. As he described it, their romance had had idyllic settings: greenwood glades and shady groves; well-leafed lanes at dusk; and murmuring streams for sitting by and tossing pebbles in on drowsy afternoons.

Her letters had stirred his memories of Jessica. She had a light but tuneful voice and her favourite song was 'She Moved through the Fair'. I knew. I'd heard her singing its melancholy lyric, 'it will not be long love 'til our wedding day'. She loved whist but would cheat at patience, turning cards over out of sequence and moving columns around shamelessly. Once into a book, she would screw up her forehead in concentration, at times not hearing others speak. She baked truly wonderful scones. Her riding was top hole and better than his, in fact they'd really first become close one hunting afternoon when she had led his horse back after Billy had fallen and was nursing his knee. Naturally, she'd always been around but for some reason he'd never taken any notice of her, they'd never really talked of anything before. She made him laugh, she did the cruellest and most killing imitations of people and she could be most amusingly coarse for one so ladylike. Her stallion Satan was sought after to cover the mares for miles around and she would talk to Satan about the mares as if he could understand, ask him how he'd found them, which had been the best and so on.

Billy and I strolled under the trees and with our tunics off lolled in the shade in shirt sleeves, with only the distant rumble of guns to tell us we were still at war. When he spoke of Jessica, that first smile of hers by the roses filled my mind. Constance's face was nowhere. I found Billy's talk and my incipient envy both excruciating and exciting. The way he spoke of her and of certain places they'd explored led me to assume that they were lovers. Perhaps Billy wanted to give me that impression, young men commonly do, but much later Jessica tearfully told me otherwise.

"My mother said he'd never marry me if I did. It was my lever, she said. Now every moment of the day I wish I had. Such a small a thing to have done."

Some days after my excursion with Billy, I walked alone through pine-woods, a mulch of needles underfoot, a breeze through the branches overhead, far from the war at Paris-Plage, which I ventured to from 24 General Hospital at Etaples, where I was sent after my own crash.

We were a fairly good crash brigade all told in our squadron and three of us wrecked our machines that same day, though there were extenuating circumstances. A gale was blowing and merely to take off was difficult enough but the Aussies were attacking and needed our help. As we bombed and strafed the Hun trenches, the west wind buffeted us, throwing our fragile SEs up in the air and casting us down again, an absolutely terrifying experience while flying at two hundred feet.

I was low down and making very slow progress against the sixty mile an hour wind when over the engine's roar, I was confused to hear what sounded like branches tapping against a window. I glanced around and saw rents appearing in the lower wings and too late, for I heard the engine miss, threw the bus over to be swept at a hundred and sixty miles an hour away from the machine gun I must have been virtually stationary above. The engine continued to miss and I could only turn again and point the SE towards the lines and hope that nothing else vital was hit as we laboured back, far too low for safety, my speed reduced to forty miles an hour in the teeth of the wind.

I was not far over the enemy side but a very anxious two or three minutes followed. I was willing the engine on, expecting that at any moment it would seize up, and searching the sky behind and above in case a Hun had spotted me, while waiting for a bullet from one of the dozen machine guns below that must be firing at me.

Finally I crossed the lines but kept on with one eye all the time on likely open spaces to left and right until I reached our field. Someone else was landing so I did a circuit and was pleased to spot chaps running out of the mess to see who was coming back with such a dickey sounding motor. Coming over the hedge I switched off and looked over the side so that, as I had been taught, I could touch down when individual blades of grass became distinguishable.

When I woke up I was lying next to a pile of wood and olive drab fabric, surrounded by flying boots and puttees. A sudden crosswind, they told me later, had taken the powerless SE and cartwheeled it across the field. Something: gun butt, Lewis gun magazine, stone, had knocked me cold. 'A5924' was a write off.

Afterwards I felt sorry about it since it was the best bus I flew in France. It had taken me high and flown me low without complaint until I steered it through a machine gun barrage.

My head was splitting and I couldn't count the doctor's fingers, so they packed me off to Etaples. On the second day, I passed their test by standing unsteadily on one foot with both eyes shut. I could only hold my breath for sixty seconds though and couldn't blow the mercury up too high, the result it seemed of altitude flying, so the doctor prescribed seaside walks and the rest of the week flirting with the nurses.

It was delicious to have no duties and to be able to depend on being alive tomorrow but more delicious still was to be among women again. I can remember to this day, lying in the darkened ward, listening to whispered voices passing down the corridor as the day nurses went off duty; waiting expectantly to hear a gurgled laugh or a stifled giggle. They were such warm and human sounds after engines and machine guns and so exciting that I couldn't sleep for images of Jessica in her hospital, where her uniformed flank stretching across a bed to tuck in sheets must surely be arousing other people's lust; where her laughter must be the cause of other men's insomnia. I didn't say any of that to Billy but I remember waxing lyrical when I got back to the squadron on the tonic that nurses were to the war effort.

Billy seemed immediately different. It was my absence let me see the change. Had I stayed at the squadron those ten days I would never have noticed it but I returned revived and his deterioration was clear. He was quieter, yet somehow more noisy; more casual but more intense. He would stare through the window at nothing and then suddenly jerk into life, casting around for someone to have fun with. His nails had gone, bitten to the quick and he smoked incessantly. His ragging in the mess was much less subtle; there was less humour and more destruction. One of the new men, younger even than us, whose name I hadn't learnt, foolishly opened a package in the mess. It was a birthday gift, chocolates from his mother. Billy snatched it from his grasp and whirled it around the room, vainly pursued by the new man as the chocolates left the box for people's mouths. The man gave up the chase and stared at Billy, close to tears I thought.

It was a scene from a public school story, a scene one might have called horrific if the war had not already grabbed that adjective entirely for itself. Though later I saw Billy lead the victim off for tennis and heard him tell the new man what a sport he was to take a joke like that, in the instant that Billy snatched the box I didn't recognise him. This was new and out-of-character behaviour. I felt responsible somehow, as if I had deserted him by slacking at the sea; allowing him to do my dirty work and suffer the consequences while I was sitting under pine trees holding hands with nurses on their days off.

Round about this time, Billy shot down a German. We were already credited with two or three fractions, having joined in and fired at Huns which the flight had shared.

But this one was all his own. He seemed frightfully bucked and was vicious at mess rugger that evening and had to go around later scrounging to replace the chairs he broke but the different tone of the conversation we had in the dark that night is borne out by his diary entry.

Sept 15th:

Feel dreadfully poo-poo when I should be feeling bright having got a Hun today. We were following Mitch at his usual hide and seek among the clouds, tracking something only he had seen, when three Fokkers popped up ahead of us and didn't realise we were there. The one in front of me was only twenty yards away so finally I was close enough to hit something and as a reflex I shot at it. It had a green tailplane, a kind of shimmering emerald in the sunshine and a girl's name, 'Eloise', was written in white letters two feet high under the cockpit on top of the lozenge camouflage. I kept firing because I couldn't miss and then the Fokker seemed to twitch, the nose went up, then down and the pilot turned round to look at me and pulled his helmet off as if he needed air. His face had a puzzled expression and he stared at me for a moment before his head fell to one side and so did the Fokker. It fell into a spin and the name 'Eloise' tuned away from me until I picked it out again on the Fokker's next turn below me. I knew I'd killed him and he wouldn't pull out. All the way home I saw that puzzled face staring at me and I remembered Jem turning my gun away from the kingfisher when I was twelve and I imagined 'Eloise' opening one of those telegrams.

"He'd have done it to you," I'm sure I told him from behind my glowing cigarette that night. "You were lucky, you saw him first and what's the difference anyway between him and those poor devils we bomb in the mud all the time?"

"What a weary waste it is," he wrote to end his diary entry.

Of course, it was a weary waste and thanks to Sassoon, Graves, Owen and Co. the whole world later knew it was but at the time what alternative was there? The war had caught us up. We'd been cast in this absurd comedy and couldn't shrug off the role we'd each been given to perform, though for pilots there was another way out perhaps.

If war for most was boredom interspersed with terror, for us terror remained but comfort replaced boredom. You might think terror would seem a reasonable price to pay for our escape from squalor but our terror, in fact, was very hard to bear. Daily we crossed the lines and within minutes found ourselves the targets of Fokkers, Archie or machine guns from the ground. Instantly we became the prey of squirming fear. Then, in another instant, the terror would flee as we re-crossed the lines back again to our comfortable world of baths and beds and wine with dinner. What a contrast! And what an adjustment that we had to make once, twice or sometimes three times a day.

Our "other way out" would be to cross the lines and land in a quiet spot where we could burn machine and find the nearest German soldier. It happened genuinely everyday as it had almost happened to Billy. One would impose no more telegrams on German girlfriends nor ever again experience that awful night long dread, waiting for dawn and the first soft tap at the door that was meant to wake you up.

It's early now, no light outside. The computer I use sits bathed in lamplight on my desk and I'm working on it at the time of day at which I used to rise to fly. No one's woken me though, unless it's death that has. We buried my good friend Tom yesterday. He was an old sweat like me, though twenty years my junior. His six medals came from the war after mine. The ladies were upset and so was I. We all loved him. He was tall and silver-haired. A mine of wit and information, he wore his learning lightly. He's another I've outlived. His death kept this machine switched off for days until last night the radio told of soldiers in the Great War shot by firing squad for cowardice. The anger and the pity that boiled up in me have driven me back to my desk.

Three hundred and seven men, after bombardment or sometimes years in the trenches, became good for nothing as soldiers, usually though plain exposure to the awfulness of the war. Most were shot without real investigation or understanding of their situation. Their sentences were ratified from desks deep in chateaux by Rawlinson or Haig or their like, who felt obliged to stop the rot; to encourage the others.

A parade of ghosts marched though my room then: Keble, Baker, Thomson, Davidson, Butcher, Smart, Daly, Bright, Tugwell, Evans, MacKinley, Hamilton,

Taylor, Winter, Oughton, Hassal, Roope, Brown, Rooney, Cameron, Kennington and waves of rage swept though me for my dead comrades and for those unknown executed men, more than one a week throughout the war, who did not have our chance to leave the mud and squalor.

But what am I saying? War is hell? Well, we all know that. And it still is. I know little more about the subject except that old men make wars and young men fight them. But the men whom I was young and at the war with didn't know what was to come and so I must remember that it was a lark too sometimes. There were the pig races that Billy and our Yank in 'B' Flight, Daly, organized; noisy card games like slippery sam; inter-squadron football and rugby, which despite the viciousness displayed unfortunately produced no injuries that would prevent flying. Finally but perhaps most important, there were the frequent squadron binges that usually ended in free-for-alls and broken furniture.

We were nineteen or twenty or twenty-one. We had no families or attachments to restrain us. We spent a good part of each day at the most tense activity there was; trying to kill while avoiding death ourselves. Tension would snap us if not released, so singing, shouting, running, cheering, gambling, fighting, hooliganism were the order of the day and the major, our ringleader, was usually found at the bottom of whatever pile of bodies our festivities degenerated into. I suppose he needed these diversions too. It was him who gave the orders and except for one occasion he always sprang a binge when somebody went down.

The day that Mitch didn't return, the major flew till dusk, low down on the other side, looking for wrecks. Our Archie had reported a lone SE surrounded by Huns. It had been seen to crash. The major forbade all but one of us to accompany him. We sat in silent groups till he and Burke taxied in out of the gloom.

"Nothing," he said and went to the mess and stared through the window into the darkness.

I'd never known the squadron so affected by a death.

"Who will protect me now?" I remember thinking. Billy's face seemed to express the same question.

"If Mitch can't survive, what chance for us," was I'm sure the squadron's one unspoken thought. Billy's confidence fled from that day but I've often wondered how he might have fared if the news had come a day or two sooner than it did, that Mitch was down and safe, or almost so, on the other side.

Some years later, I read Mitch's version of that last flight in his memoirs, which I found in an L.A. book store in the late twenties when the war was back in fashion, just before he flew his mail plane into Lake Michigan in a snowstorm. Mitch wrote:

My engine had been playing up, I took off to test the plugs and put it through its paces. I crossed the lines at fifteen thousand feet having seen a two-seater in the distance but he must have spotted me for he made off straight away. Then some of our Archie came up near me and led off east towards a mass of circling dots below at ten thousand feet. I put my nose down and quickly made out an RE8 turning for all it was worth, surrounded by five or six Fokkers getting in each other's way as they tried to shoot it. Our unwritten rule was to join any fight under any circumstances when our machines were outnumbered, so though I hated doing it because it went against all the laws of caution I'd developed, I went straight for them. It was our job to look after our two-seaters and poor old Harry Tates were easy meat at the best of times.

I got one straight away that turned and flopped and spun away, gushing smoke. The second one I shot at turned on its back and dived vertically. I thought I'd got him too but I couldn't watch because the others were splitarsing like mad and I had to watch my tail. The Harry Tate must have made a bee-line for the lines while the Huns were occupied because I didn't see him again. I got behind a Hun with a yellow tail and yellow wing tips. He could fly that Hun but eventually I got a burst though his cockpit and he slid off sideways and spun down.

I pulled away and was changing the drum on the Lewis gun when splinters flew out of the instrument panel in front of me and I felt a punch in my left arm. I flung the stick over and the world revolved. I got a stiff neck watching behind and my left arm wouldn't move but as another Hun appeared in front of me, I fired straight at his cockpit and saw the pilot's head go down. Then I must have passed out till I woke up spinning, nearer the ground. The engine sounded sick as I pulled out. Holes appeared in my starboard lower wing and I turned away from them. There was smoke coming from the engine and I figured I'd be a flamer and was done for so I flew straight at the Fokker that was chasing me, thinking I'd take him down, too.

I guess he thought I was a goner and was too surprised to manoeuvre. At the last moment I fired and he burst into flames. I passed out again and I came to nearer the ground and on my own. My left leg was covered in blood. Looking for somewhere to put down, I saw a gun emplacement ahead and cocked my gun to shoot but then thought better of it. I guess that was a smart move, for those were the guys that pulled me out and saw me to a casualty clearing station.

Mitch's Victoria Cross came through after the war when the full details of his flight were known but we learnt what had happened from the Archie battery that had counted the Germans going down, though we had to wait for weeks until we heard that Mitch had lived.

Billy grew reckless. On our next patrol, he hit a Hun, a Pfalz, and followed him down. Thorpe, our new flight commander, shot another off his tail and was rightly furious on our return.

"Height is everything," he insisted, just like Mitch. But it didn't come across in the same way. Thorpe was short and thickset with a sparse ginger moustache. He was experienced and certainly wise in the ways of the air but he talked of "Jimmy", meaning McCudden and "Mick" meaning Mannock, whom he'd trained with, in such a way that people raised their eyebrows at each other as he turned his back. Of course, no one could have filled Mitch's shoes but after that generous, exuberant but modest nature, hot air seemed all the harder to accept.

"He's got some crust, that bloke," Billy complained

as we waddled away in our flying suits. He was resentful and low, elation at his second Hun fled.

"He was right, Billy. Mitch would have said the same."

"Not you as well, George!"

Billy put it in his diary. But he didn't change his ways.

I later understood that taking risks was a recognized reaction to fear. When a pilot knew he was terrified, he couldn't acknowledge his fear by tempering his flying to account for it, since others might see and know. Therefore, hell for leather into the thick of it, banish thought, no one will think I'm frightened if I dive straight at the Hun.

Years later, I read of another reaction. A flight commander ordered on a dangerous flight, who didn't feel able to undertake it and told his CO that. When informed of the alternative, to be stripped of wings and rank and sent down the line, he lit a pipe in the latrines and blew his brains out. Harold Balfour told that tale and couldn't understand why the man could not take his chance on life by making the flight. I, in my turn, couldn't understand why Billy had thrown caution to the wind.

"It's fate, George," he would say. "If my name's on the bullet, it will get me. What can I do? And it's the only way I can keep control. If I think, I'm done for."

I have one strange, strong memory of him then, just before his death. He was in a tree, leaning against a branch, plucking apples to toss down to me. We'd volunteered to scrump for the mess one gloriously dud afternoon. Level with my eye, braced in the fork of the trunk, was his brown shoe, shiny from a batman's care, bearing spots of rain that failed to soak into the polished surface.

Ask me for an image of that age and I would conjure up those polished brown shoes. Men still wore them then and did for many years to come but then there were gentlemen still, like Billy, and on the sufferance of the King's commission, myself, who wore but did not polish them. Later, you had to polish them yourself, for the great underclass which polished other people's shoes had gone. Now of course we all wear moulded rubber and plastic and in this home for the superannuated I press down the Velcro tabs and slop around in trainers, so easy on the pedal extremities.

How Billy's father in his hand-made Oxford's would have gawped!

Six

Over the previous months we'd begun to win the war I discovered later from reading accounts of my battles. Of course, we knew that even then because we had to fly a little further each day to find the front line. Our generals had learnt the errors of their ways and no longer gave a two week warning bombardment before attacking but instead crept silent through the morning mist to surprise the Hun, or rather sent their troops to do so. On 8th August it had started and gone steadily on since then. If we could only live long enough, we would emerge victorious.

But Thorpe went down, shot from the ground as we escorted DH9s dropping ammunition to our advance troops. "Poor Thorpe is gone," Billy wrote in his diary, "and I wished him so after he bawled me out and now I feel responsible. It was only his job, as mine was to follow him. Will it ever end? Tomorrow a balloon."

It was what we had so far avoided. Other flights had done them but we had always flown above to keep the Fokkers off. Observation balloons were as much the eyes of the enemy as photo-reconnaissance two-seaters were, but if destroying two-seaters could be dangerous, attacking balloons seemed suicidal. Archie could sit all around a balloon and point straight up. Attackers had to fly through a barrage to reach their target. It was very dangerous and the cause of much wind-up. Balloon strafers carried incendiary bullets to set the hydrogen alight. Of course, if incendiary bullets hit human flesh, the results would be horrific and if you were brought down on the other side with that on board, old sweats claimed, the Hun would execute you on the spot. Those selected for a balloon were hence the subject of much ragging.

It was a Tuesday. 24th September my logbook states, but now a real prize. Hidden all those years, tucked between its pages, I found a letter yesterday from Pippa. I will phone and tell her. There's a picture, too, of a house and clouds and sun. The sky is all along the top as children think it should be; large flowers ring the house, daffodils I think, at least they're tall and yellow; and high above the house, silhouetted against some clouds, fly two biplanes. One is larger than the other, Billy's I imagine to match his uncle's status but below the picture, encouraged probably by Constance, is a short letter from Pippa to me.

Dear Lt. Bridge,
How nice it was to meet you. I hope you are well and safe. This is a picture of you and Uncle Billy in your

airoplans over our house. It is raining today but I have
drawen the sun out as it is more chery, do'nt you think?
I can read now. Mother asks to be rememembered to
you.
Yours faithfuly,
Miss Philippa Love

It makes me chuckle now. Then, who knows? But I kept it safe and certainly would have sent her back a note, probably complimenting her on her 'new' skill of reading.

There were clouds that Tuesday, as in Pippa's picture, and we doubtless stood out against them from the ground as we crossed the lines at twelve thousand feet with 'C' flight above to guard us from attack. There were two balloons we had to go for. Billy and I were chosen. With balloons you could go in low and climb, hoping to surprise, or dive straight down through the Archie. That was the quicker route and the one we chose.

We got them. Billy's instantly caught fire; mine slowly decompressed and burnt just above the ground. I was told that later. I didn't see it. I was flat out for the lines by then, hoping nothing vital had been hit during that screaming, rackety, terrifying dive through the fuzzy brown shell bursts that swelled lazily in front of me and then shot past at the speed of light. I crouched behind the reassuring bulk of the engine, which could accommodate flying pieces of metal infinitely better than I could, and tucked my shoulders in as far as possible. My face almost touched the cockpit rim as I peered down the gun sight and watched the swollen brown balloon envelope grow before me and saw it absorb the incendiary bullets I was pouring into it with no effect.

Sitting here in my chair by the window, if I close my eyes, the rain across the glass has vanished but those great fuzzy brown shell burst blotches rise lazily towards me still and I can hear again the cacophony of engine, guns, shells and screaming wires. When I landed, I threw up. I passed it off as caused by buffeting in the air but it was wind up really. Billy, the immaculate flier, tipped his bus on its nose in the corner of the field. There were tears and holes from shrapnel in the canvas of our wings. Billy's face was white and drawn as the recording officer took our report. The major was pleased and marched us off for a scotch. "Stout work, you chaps!" he would have said.

In those last few days before he died, Billy smoked incessantly and gnawed his fingernails. He prowled the mess, stared through the windows and snapped at people for no apparent reason.

"This funk is hell," he wrote. "I swore at poor Telfer today. He's only done two jobs and asked me what the balloon was like. 'We don't discuss jobs in the mess, you bloody little Hun,' I said. I felt a wretch and apologized later."

There's a famous photograph of the French pilot Guynemer, the one who flew too high to come down as French children were told when he disappeared. The camera has caught him by surprise as he climbs into his cockpit just before his final flight. His head is cocked, alert, as if he's just heard a sound. His eyes dart off to the side, warily. Large shadows of exhaustion hang beneath them. He's a wild beast surprised by hunters. I felt a shock when I first saw that picture in a book in the thirties for though their features were different, I recognised Billy as he was when I last knew him; when we had our tiff.

Even then I didn't know how it came about, except we were both run ragged. And if I am chronicling those faults in him, those changes to the Olympian I'd worshipped, it's because he died and had no chance to alter the impression his last days made. I would have seemed the same to a third person, jerky, prickly, pale, exhausted, smoking too much. Billy should have broken a leg playing football and been rescued from his fate, as one or two lucky people were, as I was by events beyond my control but he had to go on and we argued and didn't speak for a day. Did I use his tooth powder, or his fountain pen? I took some liberty I had anyway long been allowed and Billy took umbrage.

"A chap's things are his own," he said with that haughty, rebuffing, down the nose look his breeding allowed him. That look instantly destroyed our intimacy and thrust me back into that downtrodden lower-middle class condition that my commission and Mitch's infectious, colonial, second-to-none nature had encouraged me to ignore.

I watched Billy stroll off along the edge of the field with Telfer, a Scot who always had a golf club to hand in his spare moments. I can still see Billy elegantly swinging his borrowed mashie or niblick, taking advice from Telfer, whose passion this strange game was. I seethed with rejection and, I think I could admit it even then, jealousy of Telfer. He'd usurped my place at Billy's side. Had we not been brothers, Billy and me? Was I not privy to his secrets? Had I not met Jessica? And, though he didn't know it, was I not the lover of his sister-in-law? I know I didn't form this thought so clearly then but now I recognise the true feeling I had as I watched Billy a quarter of a mile off bend towards Telfer's cupped hands to light another cigarette. Billy was mine.

More time has passed. No one has died but in telling this story I have to form my thoughts, read on in Billy's diary, consult my logbook and my journal, dredge my memory; even look at photos of those times. I have a small library and each book has its characteristics. There's the dry and informative Robertson's *Reconnaissance and Bomber Aircraft 1914-1918;* the informal McLanahan's *Fighter Pilot*, full of insights and replete with snaps of pilots shaving, having tea in deckchairs; the factual *Air VCs* by Chaz Bowyer, where Billy is number nineteen of twenty-one in the Great War section.

None of those books though describe the emotions I felt. The Ancient Spartans organised their armies in the knowledge that soldiers were attracted to each other; that each man would fight harder to save his lover's life. But what I felt so confused me that I went to the hangars and loaded ammunition drums, an activity that required no thought but would allow others.

Billy's rejection made everything seem worthless. What point to avoid a stoppage? So, I was killed – that would show him. He'd be sorry then. He'd been glad enough of my socially inept, lower middle-class company before, my words had cheered him, interested him. Well, no more of that. Let Telfer do the same if he could, this greenhorn who'd done just two jobs. If I had not been in view of air mechanics and a flight sergeant, a tear might well have sprung out onto my cheek.

When I got back to the hut, Billy was sitting hunched on his bed, a picture of misery when he looked up.

"Whatever is it?" I blurted out despite his injury to me.

"I'm so sorry, George," he said. "I'm such a wreck these days, horrible to everyone and now to you for no reason. Do please forgive me."

I know now from his diary that his golf was his apology to Telfer. "I just go around saying terrible things then have to apologise."

Well, all those cliches happened. The sun came out again. My heart leapt.

"It's the war," I said.

"I think it is," he said.

Then we talked or rather he did and I listened through the torrential rain now drumming on the hut roof. I knew then I was important to him because there was no one else he could tell and I listened well, as I knew from Constance. He was frightened. He longed to be away from all this. How easy it had seemed before, learning to fly on Avroes with no enemy but one's own incompetence. Now though, it was out of control. Now with the German army trying to kill him, he didn't know how he would survive, didn't believe he could. On jobs, he could try to get lost, stooge around clouds, return at the right time full of apologies, but that would only work once. Questions would be asked. The sky was full of British machines which would report an SE acting strangely. And anyway, alone in the sky you were a sitting duck.

Now Mitch was gone, who would protect us, how could we survive? Why had Mitch rescued him on the airfield raid? If he hadn't, he'd be tucked up now in a prison hut eating potato soup or whatever the Hun fed you. How could he return to Jessica like this? How could he tell her how he felt? He'd be forever different if he lived. Perhaps it would be better to be killed?

Having reached my great age, I know now that confessions such as those to a woman who loves you are more likely than not to bind her to you more strongly than ever. I'm sure that would have been the case with Jessica, especially if he carried on and did his job as he was doing; two and a half Huns and a balloon so far.

"I had my pistol out once to finish it," Billy said.

"But there's always a chance," I said, "no matter how terrible the job is."

"It's the uncertainty," he said.

"No, you're just suffering from a realistic appreciation of the risks allied to an over sensitive imagination. You're no coward. You're always the first to dive at Huns. Remember poor old Thorpe telling you off."

"But if I don't turn towards them instantly, I know I'll turn away, so I have to go at them. It seems like courage but it's really fear."

"What rot," I said and put my arm around his shoulder. I remember his face turning to look down at mine, just a few inches away. There were dark bags under his eyes and a razor rash on his cheek. His blond hair hung poetically adrift.

If this were a Channel 4 screenplay, at this key emotional moment we would have kissed. But it was 1918 and despite his years at Eton, where such things were no doubt rife, and mine at grammar school, where they were not unknown, we merely gazed, emotionally content in our loving brotherhood, physically content with a squeezed shoulder, till he smiled an imitation of his gold-toothed pirate's smile of yore, and I said,

"No more jobs today with all this lovely rain. Let's have a drink."

At the mess there were letters. Billy's from Jessica threw him into a deeper gloom.

"She thinks I'm a hero," he said and went to the bar.

Constance's to me was affectionate. She didn't brand me a hero but spoke of "after the war", as if there might be such a time. War news was good, she said. The map in that day's *Times* showed enormous advances. We would soon come marching home. She was in London now the Gotha bombing raids had ended. In someone's drawing room she had met Marie Stopes, famous or notorious author of *Married Love*. She admired her tremendously. She had been so fascinating and so clever. She was married to an RAF officer, actually the brother of A.V. Roe, the man who built the Avroes we had trained on. Such a coincidence, Constance remarked.

Our new flight commander, Pinner, had arrived. He was from an ex-Naval squadron, wore the old Navy uniform and gave strange flat salutes. He spoke quietly and presented considered answers with a smile that inspired confidence. He wasn't sure how many Huns he'd got, seven or eight he thought, but he didn't really count them, it didn't matter he said, it was the flight, the squadron that was important, the job they did and how many got back, not who got Huns, as long as Huns were got.

I thought we might have found our own "Auntie".

"But he isn't Mitch," Billy said in the hut, in the dark from behind his glowing cigarette.

"Mitch saw everything; he'd take you into a fight with the advantage."

"But he wanted to score," I said. "He'd take a chance. Maybe Pinner will be more cautious."

The difference between Mitch and Pinner was what I later discovered von Richthofen called the difference between hunter and shooter. Pinner was an experienced and careful pilot and leader. He would be very difficult to surprise in the air and very difficult to shoot down. He would perform his jobs conscientiously and well but would shoot Huns down only infrequently. Perhaps he didn't see it as his function, perhaps he didn't fly close enough, perhaps he couldn't shoot straight but perhaps, and this is what I suspect, because I felt it myself and I believe Billy did too, he didn't really want to. That was the difference, the difference between hunter and shooter. Richthofen, Mitch, Mannock, Ball were hunters, the rest of us were shooters. In our squadron, of all our victories, Mitch scored half. The rest of us together only scored what Mitch did. It was the same with the other hunters in their squadrons.

"Of course," Mitch had said when we asked him how he did it, "I've never really minded killing people."

The major led next day with Pinner along to learn this area of the lines. We dropped bombs on trenches near Chaulnes then climbed to patrol height. There were Huns about, who didn't care to fight. We spent an hour manoeuvring and climbing. The major was trying to get between the Huns and their home. It was an anxious time, wondering if guns would work, listening for a catch in the sound of your engine.

We cruised at around nineteen thousand feet. The engines of one or two of our SEs weren't happy at this great height and their tails hung down like those of dying fish. My fingers and toes became blocks of ice as I constantly scanned the horizon for specks, flashes of sunlight on wings; hoping to spot any new enemy first. An aeroplane head on was only visible a mile or two away, so even at our stalling speed of sixty miles an hour, we would meet in one minute; very little time to think, cock guns, prepare. Combined with the cold and the oxygen starvation we were suffering, which aviation medicine had barely begun to consider, the tension was very difficult to bear. I could see the Huns the major was stalking but I was more worried by the ones I couldn't see who might be stalking us, so I constantly looked back and, though in formation, I jinked and banked every thirty seconds or so, searching the sky around, so much of which was hidden from me by the wings, the nose and tail.

I've often since thought how primitive this warfare was, like Jew and Philistine taunting each other from opposite hills, waiting for Goliath's challenge to be taken up; and how quickly this fighting reduced itself to man against man; a terrifying duel of skill and courage, so different from the slow trudge below through mud and machine gun bullets fired by an unseen, impersonal enemy. Even its popular name, dog fighting, emphasized its individuality. So at any moment poor little me might be faced by the charge of a berserker who, through uncanny inhuman knowledge, would have selected me as the weakest link in our defence. As I said, the tension in this waiting game was enormous.

I cocked my guns and fired a few rounds to test them. The Huns were a mile south-west of us and a thousand feet below when the major rocked his wings and took us down. As I glanced behind one last time before concentrating on the enemy, I saw Billy's SE drawing away to the right, diving but leaving us. I followed the major's lead as he pulled up slightly, obviously having noticed Billy. I scanned the sky below. Had Billy seen a better target? Or spotted a danger? Seeing nothing though, I followed the major as he put his nose down again and I lost sight of Billy. We fell upon the Huns. Given time, they'd turned towards us. As usual I didn't hit anything and a gaudy Albatros flashed past me. The major's target smoked then broke up into a tumbling collection of wings and fabric. As we followed the major straight home, for we'd been out long and were well over Hunland, we left the long smudge of his victim trailing from eighteen thousand feet almost to the ground. Of Billy, there was no sign, until we reached the field and saw his SE on the ground.

When I came out of the hut with the idea of finding someone who would play bridge with me, I almost walked into Pinner with his arm through Billy's. Pinner took my arm on his other side. "I'm rounding the chaps up for a chat," he said. When we reached his hut, we met the others of our flight already gathered there.

He wanted to get to know us, wanted to make sure we got to know each other he said as we drank his whisky, ranged around his hut on beds, chairs and table.

"Now study Love and Bridge, you other blokes," he said. "They've been out here two and a half months and they're just getting to be useful, no disrespect to them, and you can all learn something from them."

Billy and I were in fact the senior members of the flight with Butcher, Baker and the others gone.

Tugwell, Kennington, Cameron and Telfer were replacements since the squadron had come out. Billy or I would lead patrols on Pinner's day off.

Pinner ran through the signals he would use in the air then reached the real point of the gathering.

"Love made a mistake today," he said.

"Damn stupid," Billy said, glancing round, then down at his shoes.

"His Vickers jammed and he went home at the wrong time. The major's bawled him out about it. He should have gone immediately he realized he couldn't fix it, or stayed without it. He had his Lewis gun working. Now, I don't think you should stay twenty miles over with just a Lewis gun. We all know how difficult it is to change a drum in the middle of a fight, so I think Love should have left at once."

"I thought we might not get amongst the Huns, in which case I'd be all right." Billy looked around at us again for understanding.

"Instead," Pinner went on, "he left at just the wrong moment. None of us knew what was going on. I thought he'd spotted another group coming at us. He threw our attack off and gave the Huns time to turn to meet us. We might have lost someone ourselves and where we might have got four or five, we only got one. So scouts, in that situation, either leave early or don't leave at all."

Our meeting ended but Pinner wanted to be shown the area, so he led Billy to the hangars. Five minutes later, they took off. As Pinner left the ground, he went into an immediate climbing turn. New senior arrivals usually did something like that to demonstrate their skill, to make their mark on the troops. Then he flew back across the field and did a slow roll at two hundred feet before climbing to join Billy who was circling a thousand feet above him.

The major had doubtless destroyed Billy in his office and Pinner was now busy building him up again: the aerial tour, including lots of stunting and contour chasing; the open discussion of jammed guns and wrong decisions; the suggestion that the others should look up to him and me; the arm in arm stroll. Perhaps it was merely what we would now call psychology but I found myself liking Pinner enormously.

Billy's last diary entry, uncharacteristically short, said only: "Gun jammed, home early. Stunting with Pinner. Nice cove."

But as he washed that evening, collar off, braces hanging, while I tried again to progress with *Howards End*, he said into the mirror: "The major found me out. He said I'd be off the squadron directly if it happened again. My gun did jam!" Billy said.

"Well, then," I laid the book down and looked at his reflection.

"But I knew I should have stayed or gone sooner as Pinner said. I could have dived straight through them, a quick squirt with the Lewis and enough rounds to get home safe with."

He dried his face and sat on the end of my bed.

"It was just funk. But all that jockeying for position! We were buzzing around for an hour! If we'd gone straight in, I'd have been fine."

"The buzzing around keeps us alive," I said.

"But the wait is so awful. Looking behind you all the time. Wondering where a bullet's going to come from. Do you think I should pack it in? See the major?"

At the time I was certain I knew what Billy wanted to hear me say and it came out pat.

"What about Jessica and your family?"

He looked so mournful that I sat up and patted his shoulder.

"Come on, Billy, we'll have a drink and it will feel all right. One day at a time will soon build into weeks, then months and before we know it the days will be much shorter and it'll be December. They'll send us home for leave and six months instructing, then send us back in Snipes next autumn and we'll run rings round the Hun."

"December!" Billy laughed. "It's September 28th. Two months! Three months!" He seemed to find it funny and laughed again. "That's a lifetime."

After dinner, a binge looked like developing. 'B' Flight on their evening patrol had surprised five Huns and sent the lot down. They all felt they were jolly good fellows and lorded it around the mess until someone squirted them with a soda siphon and general mayhem ensued. I went outside to smoke, listening to the rumble of guns and wondered how we'd all be feeling if 'B' Flight had disappeared en masse as those Huns had from their mess.

Pinner came out.

"Squadron show tomorrow, Bridge. Ten ack emma,

the major leading. We've got to nursemaid a balloon for God's sake. Some general or someone wants to see the lines for an hour without getting his boots muddy!"

The major was furious next morning.

"Wing says it must be Haig or the Prince of Wales or some such nincompoop, Brigade won't let on," he said. "They've put two squadrons on it. They're livid about it but it's come down from the top against all protests. We're to stay above and make sure nothing gets through. Nothing!"

The plan was idiotic. With the best will in the world no one could guarantee to protect a balloon and strangely, the more machines there were in the air, the more difficult protection would become since we'd all get in the way of each other. Given this responsibility though, the Colonel at Wing HQ couldn't just say to his regular patrols, "Keep an eye out for balloon busters, chaps." He had to put up special protection.

It was 29th September. A Sunday. Unusually, the sun was shining. As we gathered by our machines, mechanics were cleaning out the hangar set aside for the church service scheduled for 3 pm. Our ten o'clock take off to war would not interfere with that. People were nervous, as normal, though we were always happier about squadron shows, since to be one of eighteen or twenty machines up together produced a feeling of security, even if it was somewhat illusory.

Billy had been at the sheds early, checking ammunition because of his gun jam the day before. He looked pale, and smoked until the major signalled us to climb in and start engines.

'A' Flight had drawn the short straw. We would be the low level protection in case someone sneaked in. It would mean stooging around near the lines at seven or eight thousand feet, within a mile of the balloon, while 'B' and 'C' Flights, led by the major, would be stacked above, watching the heavens. First though, since the major found it immoral to use so much fuel without adding to the Hun's misery, we would all cross the lines and drop bombs.

We took off and made first for the balloon's site three miles or so behind the lines. It was sitting on the ground below ready for its ascent at 10.45, grey and fat like a beached whale as we flew over it. We crossed the lines at perfect Archie height and brown woolly shell bursts duly appeared.

Pinner led us in dive and zoom, turn and bank but we were essentially target practice. I could see 'B' and 'C' Flights untroubled above us and hoped the Sopwith Dolphins planned for high protection were up at twenty thousand. To my relief, Pinner quickly unloaded his bombs on some support trenches and we all followed suit. We flew back to the balloon and on cue it began to rise. Soon after that, Hun telephones would have been red hot as they reported this strange aerial activity around a balloon that must be of supreme tactical importance.

We circled the balloon and sometimes as a variation flew away and then turned to make the run back. At the end of a run Pinner would bank to turn. When a flight turned together, the machines on the outside had to gun their engines since they had further to fly in the same time. This was wearing for pilots and engines, so it was customary for pilots on the inside and outside of turns simply to swap sides, to fly more or less a straight line rather than a turn, to fly the chord rather than the arc of the turning circle, thus flying a shorter distance and not getting left behind. It was a manoeuvre that needed some practice. As Pinner turned this time, Cameron and Kennington flew their chords but Kennington's machine must have hit an air pocket suddenly since it dropped into Cameron's path. Before Cameron could do anything, his propeller had chewed off Kennington's tail and the two machines became locked together momentarily until Cameron's tore free and the nose fell. He seemed to have got away with it but Kennington's machine, now just a nose with wings, went straight down. Then, Cameron's top wing fluttered off as he dived for earth and he fell into a vicious spin from which there could be no escape.

I glanced around and behind. Mesmerised by this horror I had been neglecting safety. Pinner circled the spot where Kennington had gone in. There was nothing we could do but resume our patrol. I stared at the balloon, willing it to descend. Surely twenty minutes was long enough for sight-seeing. My mouth was dry and what with the Archie and the accident, for two pins, I would have flown straight home.

Then bursts of white British Archie came up nearby: the signal for Huns. Dropping down on us, with 'B' Flight tearing after them, were six Fokker biplanes. Pinner turned to meet them and though at a disadvantage, our motors dragged us up towards them.

I would have cocked the Vickers, straining my neck to hold my head forward to see through the ring and bead sight as the Fokkers grew in size. Then to my left and just ahead, I saw the underside of Billy's wings appear as he flipped over and dived away. The rest of us were among the Fokkers and turning. There were ten of us and only six of them, each occupied with an SE.

I pulled off to look around for other dangers and I spotted Billy far below, nose down, on his way to earn his Victoria Cross. His citation tells the story.

Ordered to provide close escort to an observation balloon carrying a very distinguished passenger, 2nd Lt. Love's flight was turning to face an attack by six enemy aircraft, when Love, alone of all his flight, spotted a low level intruder making for the balloon. Without a thought for the danger of diving away from attacking hostile aircraft which also enjoyed a height advantage, Love made straight for the enemy. No gunfire was heard by the balloon commander, so it is assumed that Love fired off all his Lewis gun ammunition early in an attempt to alert the German pilot and divert him from his intention and that his Vickers gun jammed at this crucial moment as had happened on the day before. In his high speed dash, 2nd Lt. Love would have had no time to change the drum on his over wing Lewis gun.

Aware of the paramount importance of the

observation balloon's passenger and being unable to engage the attacker with gunfire, 2nd Lt. Love deliberately flew his aeroplane into the hostile machine. The collision, which destroyed both machines, threw 2nd Lt. Love from his cockpit to fall to earth just north of the balloon post.

For his selfless courage in unhesitatingly choosing the only alternative that would allow him to perform his duty, 2nd Lt. Love is awarded the Victoria Cross. His action, in the last weeks of the War was an inspiration to his squadron, the RAF and the whole army.

I had followed Billy, forlornly trying to assist and saw him catapulted from his cockpit: Icarus falling. Then sunlight caught his goggles for an instant before his body turned and I lost it against the ground. The two machines with petrol from ruptured tanks pouring over hot engines fell in one burning mass.

I circled the spot. I remembered the fight above but as often happened in air combat, the sky had emptied. The balloon was nearly down now and the VIP would soon be safely out of the basket I imagined. Smoke billowed from the wreckage as I swooped low over the ring of soldiers that had formed around it. Fifty yards away a dozen khaki figures stood in a smaller circle on some grass. I flew slowly past, thirty feet up, and hung over the side. They'd laid a groundsheet over Billy. An officer looked up at me and drew a white hand across his throat. I wanted to land but there was nowhere large or flat enough. I flew back again hoping against hope that the bundle on the ground might have moved then I spotted SEs above me. I climbed and recognised Pinner's blue streamer. I pulled in on the other side to Telfer. We cruised at a safe height above the lines. Pinner must have been watching for Huns but I saw, again and again, only the horrifying moments of the collision and Billy's turning body, the glint from his goggles a last salute, or reproach, since my encouragement had put him in the air that morning. Was he alive or dead when he fell? Did he have that conscious half minute to contemplate his end?

An orderly called me to the major's office as I sat alone in the hut later, staring at the wall. The major looked embarrassed.

"Bridge, did Love tell you about the other day?"

He poured out whisky.

"I can't apologise to him but I can to you. It was a damn fine thing he did and I was obviously wrong. I'd like to drink his health. You're not to fly again today."

I mooched over to the mess and fellows came up to me quietly in ones and twos as at a funeral to commiserate and to congratulate me on Billy's behalf. I told the story again and again at their bidding.

Wing knew all about it and the balloon commander and observer phoned and would send reports. The major at a distance had seen everything as he pulled up from finishing his Hun. Encouraged by the balloon's passenger, whom Billy's action had deeply impressed but who was still not identified, nor ever was for reasons of security, the major prepared another VC recommendation.

"It'll be a scandal if he doesn't get it," he said that night at dinner as we drank Billy's health after that of the King.

I stayed drinking so long that the hut was turning when I fell asleep. I woke with a raging thirst and emptied my water bottle. I sat up and smoked in the dark but there was no answering glow opposite, for Billy, whom I had talked into flying, now led the parade of ghosts that marched around my bed. Alone in the hut we had shared, it was a night so full of guilt and loss that I could only clutch my knees and rock back and forth as I sobbed in my desolation. Eventually I woke to heavy rain. The weather was too bad to fly and everybody else was cheerful. I went through Billy's things and packed them up.

I have only a few clear memories of that time with the squadron. I did my duty as soldiers must. We heard that Mitch was safe and my log book shows I did four more jobs. The one I remember involved a horrific chase after gun teams, ruddering into my sights horses already terrified by the roar of our engines. We came under severe ground fire and suffered many hits but we all returned.

Billy was dead and my feeling of responsibility for that returned every day after dark. Each time I opened the hut door though, I half expected to see his smile and hear his cheery "What ho, George!" from the early days as he'd look up from the diary he'd be writing. The diary lay in my drawer. I longed to open it but feared to learn things about myself and in the end resisted. Later I passed it on to Constance. I wasn't sure if Jessica would be able to bear to read it.

The weather was overcast and depressing. We scuttled out to the war and scuttled back, chased by rain that drummed on the taut canvas of our wings as we pulled ourselves from our cockpits, back in front of our hangars again. A New Zealander named Zin Zan Fuller moved in. He offered me the respect due to a deputy flight leader and the associate of a genuine hero, for all arrivals heard the story instantly. He seemed slightly awed to be occupying Billy's half of the hut. That night he woke me. A candle was burning by his bed and for a moment I thought he was Billy.

"You were shouting," he said. I sat up.

"No, I couldn't make anything out," he replied.

It was a dream that became regular over several years. I lay ill in bed and my father was hugging me, initially perhaps to give me warmth but then tighter, crushing and suffocating me till I had to struggle and fight to escape, finally shout and scream for release since he'd never knowingly injure me. Each episode of this dream was deeply harrowing, so full of guilt and injury to loved ones did I find it.

The next day the dream seemed prophetic. The major called me to his office, sat me down, warned me of terrible news and passed a telegram to me. My parents had died within hours of each other from Spanish flu, God's punishment to humanity for the war many said. It killed twenty million around the world that year. I stared at the form unable to take this news in. The major thrust his tonic for all ills, a glass of whisky, into my hand.

I remember a blank mind and then confusion as I sat opposite him.

"What do I do?" I asked, realising I was in the major's hands.

"A week's leave. Get off straight away."

Later, much later, I thought how hard all this must have been for the major. A young man himself, only twenty-five, he was nursemaid and sergeant-major to younger men, who were often not much more than schoolboys. He had to issue orders that sent many to deaths about which he had then to compose tactfully phrased letters of sympathy to send to families. Now, with me, he'd had the opposite to do; tell one of his schoolboys that in the safety of England, his family had died.

For the second time in a few days, people offered quiet condolences, half envious perhaps that I was out of this for a while, even at such a desperate price.

On the train to Calais, the officers' compartments were cold, uncomfortable, and fugged with smoke. Windows were jammed, upholstery torn, floors filthy. I sat silent with my thoughts, an observer in the corner, as others enjoyed their anticipation of leave. No one else stood in the drizzle at the rail of the boat. I was parentless and friendless. Surrounded by grey sea and grey sky, with only a grey destroyer for company, a feeling of desolate loneliness settled on me until the motion of the ship in the rough sea forced others to join me and I threw up in company. My longing for death suddenly became one to save me from the nausea that drove all other thoughts from my mind.

In London, my aunt had organised everything. My father's sister, she was an elementary school teacher. It was her telephone calls that had arranged my telegram. It seemed too ironic I told her, that I, in France, should receive a telegram from London regretting the deaths of my parents.

Our front room was so small that with their coffins side by side, there was barely space to edge past the piano to stand beneath 'The Monarch of the Glen' to look down at them. That was when I felt true loneliness, for I was saying goodbye to the only people I could depend on to put my interests before their own.

It was my third funeral since going to France. The first, Mitch's German two-seater crew, had been a serious but almost festive event with no personal involvement.

Billy's was entirely different. Our dead usually fell in enemy lines but now, with the chance to mark the occasion, which might also represent many other unmarked deaths, the whole squadron plus the colonel from Wing attended. There were three graves. We buried Cameron and Kennington, too. There was a service, a firing party, a bugler to play the last post and an official photographer to record everything.

The sun poked out for a few minutes, which helped make a good picture. I have seen it in several books over the years. Billy's coffin, bearing a wreath and his cap, has pride of place over the grave. To the right are the bugler and the firing party with arms at present, then the padre in the centre, then the squadron. The major and I stand next to each other. A breeze has ballooned our trousers a little. We stand at attention, caps under our arms. Looking at this picture now, I cannot believe I was ever so young or my hair so dark, my face so tired.

When I later read of Mozart's burial, attended only by a dog, I recognised the scene at once from my parents' funeral. The day was cold, grey and drizzly. With the war and influenza, the country was stricken by deaths. My uncle Fred was dead and if alive would have been in France. My parents' cousins and their children had war work and their own worries, as also did neighbours, so though there were cards and flowers, only my aunt and I joined the vicar at the cemetery. We followed close behind another influenza victim and in turn our place was taken by a tiny white baby's coffin.

I refused my aunt's offer of accommodation and when she returned home, I found myself alone in a cold empty house full of childhood ghosts. I sat by a fire in the sitting room where my Uncle Fred had extolled the Royal Flying Corps. I managed to answer one or two letters before I felt exhausted and wandered around the house from empty room to empty room. I fell asleep in an armchair with my trench coat on top of me and woke at dawn, aching all over and guessing what was wrong.

In half an hour or so, I was locking the door behind me before staggering off to join the early commuters at the station. At eight o'clock I knocked at the door of the house in Eaton Square which I knew from her letters to be Constance's.

She later told me I looked like a corpse. I may well have done for I was shivering by then as well as aching and I had a splitting headache. I was manhandled upstairs and hot-water-bottled into bed, where I woke at times and was pronounced on by a doctor. Three days later I discovered his certificate for Spanish flu had gained me a two–week extension of leave.

I slept late, had broth for lunch, read Turgenev by the drawing room fire, napped after tea and rose again for dinner unless there was company. Then I might eat alone in my room if I did not feel energetic enough for conversation and read in bed until I fell asleep or Constance crept to join me. It would have been a good regimen to recover from the War, let alone Spanish flu, if only deaths had left me to myself.

My mother in particular I could not let go. Alone in my room, attempting to read, with my legs toasting by a fire, I would stare into the flames, hearing the evocative crack and burble of the fire and would remember my childhood; things she'd said and things we'd done together. How could I have gone to Billy's instead of seeing her longer that last time? I saw her as she read my letter of explanation and my imagination of her disappointment mortified me. I imagined her anxiety over the past three months of my active service at each unusual knock at the door, wondering if this was her telegram. Instead, I'd received the telegram. There seemed no justice in her dying and despite the randomness of death in war that I'd become accustomed to, I still sought justice in other deaths.

Sometimes Billy's face replaced my mother's in the coals. I had guilt about persuading him to fly that day which I could share with no one, since I alone was guardian of his secret. My story of his death had gelled into discreetly goreless heroism. His body had in fact been badly broken by the impact, his face so smashed by collision with the windscreen before he fell, our doctor said, that he was certain to have been unconscious when his goggles flashed that last farewell. My truthful story shocked Constance, who said, "Don't tell Hester about his face. Those two poor handsome brothers!"

When alone, I seemed to cry a lot. Perhaps it was the grey October skies and falling leaves. Perhaps Turgenev didn't help but *Three Men in a Boat* had seemed too totally removed from life for me to turn the pages. Flu and grief combined to produce a sleep inducing listlessness that kept me around the fire and further stoked my guilt. Here was I in dozy comfort, when a hundred miles away Germans chased my former comrades. I hadn't done enough of my duty to enjoy this ease I hadn't earned.

Eventually I progressed to turns around the Square and brisker walks across the Park but the medical board I attended gave me another week. "Long tramps in the country are what you need," one of the bluff old gentlemen said and I could no longer avoid a visit to Billy's.

Seven

Constance and Pippa accompanied me. Hayter met us at the station with the car in which Billy had driven us to the sea three months before. I couldn't respond to Pippa's excited chatter. I was dreading my meeting with Sir Richard and Lady Love. It was only two weeks since they'd heard of the death of their second son.

In fact of course they were calm and extremely proper. Sir Richard called me "my boy," and Lady Hester gripped my hand warmly in both of hers as she told me of her sorrow at my loss with no mention of her own. Constance had naturally kept them well-informed by telephone and letter and they knew everything that she knew but after tea, Pippa went to feed the chickens and I had to tell the story again. I muted the tone and omitted the fall and flashing goggles, which seemed too special to me and too emotionally melodramatic for others, especially his parents.

"The foolish boy, the foolish, foolish boy," Lady Love repeated, wringing a handkerchief in her hands as I told them how Billy had flown straight at the Hun and brought him down, the only one of us who'd seen, the only one who could complete our task.

"The squadron was terribly cut up," I said, "and terribly proud of Billy. The major said it was magnificent." "Ma ce n'est pas la guerre," Lady Love's eyes said to me.

Then, breeding came out as they used to say it would. She blew her nose and spoke to Sir Richard, "Let us go to find Philippa." He limped out of the room after her and remembered to square his shoulders, which had slumped a little as he stood by the fire and pretended to clean a pipe.

When I called at Jessica's house, she was in her post-hospital bath. I walked around fields and returned as dusk fell. Passing the window of the lamp lit drawing room, I saw Jessica by the fire, gazing into the flames over the book she held. I recognised her mood. But she flung the door wide for me when I rang.

"I have to have a bath immediately," she said. "I think it's the smell there. How good to see you!"

I joined her by the fire. Her book was *Wuthering Heights.*

"I can't help it," she said. "I've always loved Cathy and Heathcliff and I've had no mood for anything else since.

"They've been very polite and quite kind," she said. "Lady Love was very concerned for me, touchingly so, considering. But it's an ill wind, I suppose. Oh, I mustn't say that. I know she wouldn't think that. She would want him here whatever. I'm such a wretch!

What a thing to say! But she won't have me for a daughter-in-law now, at least, will she?

"Tell me. It was awful, wasn't it? Tell me about it. Tell me how he died. Mummy's left us alone. I told her, 'Don't come in!' I want to know. Everything, George!"

She sat on the edge of a chair with her knees together. Her brown skirt reached to the floor. Her hands were in her lap. Light from lamp and fire fell on one side of her face, throwing shadows on the other. Her hair was pulled back and tied. Her neck was slender and soft and surrounded by an open white collar. Her gaze was earnest, her eyes wide and anxious and shining in the fire and lamplight. I thought I'd never before received so trusting a look, never seen anyone so desirable.

I told my story again. I had different versions but this was the complete one that I owed to Jessica and Billy, though I confess I stressed the heroism. I stopped when she began to cry.

"He would have felt nothing," I assured her.

"I'm glad," she whispered. "At least he's not living with dreadful injuries and disfigurement like some of those poor boys at the hospital. He would have hated that."

"Would you?"

"Only for him," she said. "But was his body badly, what do you say, when someone's dead, not injured, broken?"

I told her; the fall and the gun butt.

"Oh yes, of course." She looked unblinking at me and wiped tears away with the heels of her hands.

172

"As he fell," I said, "the sunlight caught his goggles for a moment." I'd told no one, but it didn't sound foolish telling Jessica. "That brief flash," I said, "was as if he was saying goodbye to me."

"And to me," she said at once, claiming my intimacy with Billy's death for herself, "and to me," and threw her face on her knees and sobbed again.

"Oh, why didn't you save him?" she wailed. "Why did you let him die?" Her red distraught eyes stared up at me. "How can you sit there like that? Why are you here and not him?"

I stammered answers: too far away to help; Billy the only one who'd seen. Jessica wept. I fell silent. She'd hit upon the question that survivors of combat always torment themselves with and find no answer to. Why me? Why did I live through it when better men than me went down? It's vexed me all my life. I had no answer then and have none now.

"Go!" she shouted at me then, "Get out! Go away! Leave me! I can't look at you!"

I called her mother and I left. My feeling for her and for Billy had pricked tears from my eyes too as I watched her weep and wondered who there might ever be again to weep for me like that.

Jessica had welcomed me calmly then attacked me almost hysterically; she'd been a pale alluring vision then become a hideous pain-racked spectre. At nineteen I had no idea what to make of it. I believe I added more guilt to my pile as I walked back in the darkness, my footsteps on the road my only company. The trouble was, and I realised it then in the dark, that

173

despite all the sorrow, the death, despite the presence of Constance, despite my imminent return to the front or perhaps because of it, when I saw her in the lamplight with shadows and shining eyes and soft pale skin, it was Jessica I wanted to embrace, Jessica I wanted to make love to.

So, I thought, Constance wanted Richard but he was dead and so she had me. I wanted Jessica but Jessica wanted Billy, who was dead. In this arrangement of compromises, it would take but a little sideways shift to provide one heart's desire at least, mine. And let Constance go hang? A memory of Houseman's *A Shropshire Lad* tossed another chip of guilt onto those already piled high in my mind:

> *I cheer a dead man's sweetheart,*
> *Never ask me whose.*

Then Jessica called to me, clear through the darkness and far away. I stopped and answered when she called again and heard her footsteps running.

"George, where are you?" she cried, almost upon me, and I enjoyed a soft collision of cheek upon shoulder and bosom upon arm.

"Forgive me, George," she said with her hand on my sleeve. I could see only the paleness of her face held up to me in the dark.

"Come back and talk to me. I'm so ashamed to have spoken to you like that. I know you were his true friend and I've made no mention of your poor mother and father and I'm so sorry for you. I'm a beast but if you'll forgive me, we'll be friends. We must be you and I," and she swung me round and back we walked, her arm through mine as she asked me of my mother and father and we exchanged our heartbreaks.

I led a dual life in those few days I stayed at Billy's. Though I didn't turn Constance away when she crept to my room at night, during the day, when I walked the fields alone or drove to market with Constance or joined in Pippa's games or made sedate conversation with Sir Richard, I had in my mind's eye Jessica's face, her hair, her voice, the way her head turned, her smile. Those were the thoughts that transformed the day into a long exciting preparation for the evening, when she returned from the hospital.

Her work and the autumn evenings drawing in, left little time for riding and her horse languished neglected in his stall and paddock. Satan was a nickname, from his temperament, I learnt. His real name was Satin. He'd whinny in the dark as she rushed to see him on her return. His head would appear and nudge and nuzzle Jessica's shoulder, arm and breast as they communed and she'd whisper to him, stroke his cheek, blow into his nostrils or rub his neck.

I would perch on a fence, or lean and join Satan, now tied up at the door, in contemplation of his mistress hurrying about her mucking out by the light of a storm lantern placed on the courtyard flagstones. She'd bend towards us, shadows down her shirt front, or away from us, riding breeches taut across her rear. Once, glancing away from Jessica, distracted by the clop of a hoof as Satan shifted his weight, I saw a huge stallion's erection hanging beneath him. For an instant, before I laughed at myself, I felt that he must share in my desire.

Satan was a comfort to her. And since it seemed that I was a comfort too and there was now no danger of an unsuitable marriage, Billy's family was eager to help her, so Constance despatched me every evening to visit Jessica.

I found her once at patience. She announced herself stuck and I took her seat and turned the cards out in threes while casting my eyes rapidly over the sequences she'd managed. I looked up suddenly and found her gazing at me across the table with a look of such sadness on her face that I reached out at once and took her hand. It was cold but it returned the squeeze I gave it.

"How you concentrate, George," she said. "You haven't blinked or looked up once." She lifted my hand to her cheek, which was also cold.

"How warm and full of life you are. I keep imagining poor Billy in a box in the earth in France, so cold and unmoving, when he was so warm and full of life. And soon you must return and what will be left for us here when all of you young men are gone?"

Then I tempted fate by telling her of the prediction Constance had made: that I would survive. I led her to the sofa where the arm I put around her was a comfort to her till we heard her mother turn the handle of the door and we sprang apart.

The next evening, as Jessica made tea with water from the huge black kettle on the kitchen range, I watched the shadows she cast in the warm light from the lamp that stood on the scrubbed deal table I sat at. She stood by the fire that glowed through the bars as she waited for the tea to brew and did not respond as I chattered.

Could I be enough of a comfort to her, I wondered to myself; enough to help her recover from Billy's death? I remember her reflection in the black kitchen windows. She stood with her chin up, her hair pushed back and she gazed unseeing into the gloomy corner of the room. Her hands were behind her and spread to the fire, a pose that pushed out her bosom and emphasised how thin she was. The reflection was less perfect than reality but at the same time more perfect; an impression of her captured on the glass that did not show the way her nose bent, the strands of hair that had escaped her fingers as she pinned it back, the darns at the ends of her sleeves.

She poured the tea.

"Don't look at me like that, George! You look at me the way that Constance looks at you. It isn't fair. You mustn't be moonstruck."

She'd hit the nail on the head.

That afternoon Constance and I had strolled arm in arm along the sea front and she'd raised the subject of after the war. I'd mentioned flying aeroplanes since I had no other skills.

"But there are lots of things a young man can learn," Constance had suggested.

"Well, you won't have to see me look at you much longer," I told Jessica. "My medical board is on Friday, I must leave tomorrow."

I was glad in a way. My conscience was tiring me. The truth, described melodramatically, was that I was toying with Constance while infatuated with Jessica, all on the shoulders of my dead friend. I'd been in agonies during our seafront stroll since it wasn't unknown for Jessica or her colleagues to push wheel-chaired amputees and the like along the front for the sea air. Jessica would soon know all about us if we were spotted arm in arm. It seemed though that she had some concern over her own conscience for after she'd been silent for a while and I said, "You don't mind then, about my going back," she looked up at me.

"No, I'm sorry you must go back. I hope you're not really fit yet. But if you're not here, I think it might be better."

I must have looked dejected.

"George," she said, "three weeks ago I was to be married to Billy. It was all I had in my mind between his letters. There were so many things to think about; how we would live afterwards, what to make of his family, him. Now he's dead and it's all gone and I feel so sad for him and so sorry for myself. I can't see a future. All I see is these poor boys at the hospital and you gazing at me and now you have to go and I'm confused. No. Don't touch me!"

I'd stood to move round to her since she was so upset. I perched on the edge of the table. Small and demure, with her hands in her lap, she looked up at me.

"That's the worst thing of all. How can I let you

kiss me? So soon after Billy has died. When I see Billy watching us."

"He's dead," I wanted to say but didn't. Indeed, I didn't always feel that and had to tell myself he was when I kissed Jessica and my hand felt her shoulder through her dress.

"If you're gone, I'll have some time to think and make some sense of all this," she said.

"You don't want to kiss me then," I persisted.

"No. Yes. I don't know. I do but how can I want you to when it was the last thing I would have wanted three weeks ago. You're not Billy," she said using for the first time, in despair, the words that she would later taunt me with.

My board passed me fit on a Friday and I spent the Saturday wangling an SE5 to take back to avoid the boat and train. I hadn't flown for three weeks and was a little nervous that I might have forgotten how but on the apron at Lympne as I wriggled into that creaking cane seat, and waggled the control column and looked over the side along the exhausts at the fitter standing ready to swing the propeller, it all flooded back and became automatic. I found a similar thing more than twenty years later, when I hadn't flown for ten years and sat in a yellow Harvard trainer in Canada; that the feel for flying, with allowances for different machines and new cockpit layouts, didn't disappear. Once a pilot, always a pilot.

The major was pleased to see me. Two men were missing that week.

"It's good to have a pilot back who knows what he's doing, Bridge," he said, a comment that warmed me then as its memory does now.

The sound of engines brought us to the mess door, drinks in hand, and I saw the relief on his face as he counted the silhouettes of the SEs against the overcast sky and realised all were back.

The pilots I knew waved and shouted greetings but they were excited, pulling off helmets and goggles. They'd caught a two-seater and sent it down in flames. They discussed it boisterously, waving arms and sweeping hands around to imitate their machines. It was a scout pilot's dream, six against one. I felt excluded and despite the fear I knew they'd felt, even in that relatively safe fight, I envied them, wanted to be back in it, wanted to be part of the war again.

I soon was. The next evening, on Pinner's day off, I led a patrol twenty miles over and dived on a Fokker and got it: that first memory that the article about Billy's VC brought back.

Back at the field, the flight gathered round me and slapped my back, pleased to be led by a warrior hero. Zin Zan Fuller and Bright, a new man, had Huns as well as mine; three-nil. The Huns had had another pasting. They were all pleased to be led by a tactician. Zin Zan, my hut companion, basked in reflected glory too. I had to explain how I had tracked and ambushed the Huns, and thus I passed on Mitch's tuition.

In the hut that night, as Zin Zan snored, I smoked in the dark, unable to sleep. I wasn't as fearful of tomorrow as I would once have been but I remembered how months before, Billy and I had longed to dive on a Fokker and shoot one down. We had each done that and I know now from his diary that he felt as I did that November night in 1918; like a murderer and a widow-maker. I remembered the Fokker falling into a spin, its pilot dead, and I couldn't shift from my mind the image of Constance and her dead husband, and that of her father-in-law, who had burnt his son's rent and bloodied tunic so that no one should see it.

Two days later I repeated the performance, tracking and surprising a Hun patrol, getting one in flames and shooting another off Zin Zan's tail. Despite myself and perhaps only because of the poor quality of the current Hun pilots, I was a war leader and a hero. Zin Zan lauded me and the devotion began that later got me started in Hollywood. With his classic features and toothy smile, he became a star of silent films. When I needed a job, he got me one flying aeroplanes for stunts.

I did one more patrol behind Pinner on an awesome evening of huge cloud canyons shot through with pink light from the falling sun. Next day, the major cancelled our morning patrol. We stood around for two hours not quite able to believe it, listening to the rumble of guns until it stopped at the appointed moment. We variously leapt and jigged around, or as one or two of us did, stared at each other, not far from tears, silent at the thought that the war we'd lived with since boyhood had really ended and that we'd lived through it and would continue to live and that a whole new world lay open at our feet.

It was May before I was home. There was no more work for an air force except in Russia where there were still Bolsheviks to kill but since the RAF had grown in four years from five squadrons to three hundred, from a hundred aircraft to fifteen thousand, it could not be disbanded overnight, so we spent our time joyriding, playing football and writing and receiving letters.

Constance made me anxious. With Billy, my bridge to the upper classes, gone, I felt increasingly intimidated by her references to Lord So and So, Sir Peter This and Lady That, all of whom, she assured me would introduce me to someone who would have an opening. I realised in my quiet moments that I was a sixth form boy who'd learnt how to fly, how to kill and how to toast the King. I had no skills of any use to anyone and would have considered staying in the air force if the competition for permanent commissions hadn't been so great.

I needed the advice of parents of course but I had none now. My aunt supplied their missing letters and was a dedicated correspondent. I tried to match her, grateful for her kindness, and for want of subjects wrote down my thoughts and things I'd done. One letter told how I learnt to ride a horse. Zin Zan taught me on a docile nag from the neighbouring farm. In the letter, I interwove that description with one of learning to fly and then compared the two. Another letter described a routine low level sight-seeing flight in early spring over an old battlefield. Abandoned tanks and trenches and churned up earth still dominated the view but from low in the air, what was perhaps not visible from the ground could be made out, a delicate, almost shimmering haze of green, which was spreading over everything as nature reasserted itself.

We all remarked upon it, of course, but I wrote about it to my aunt. A while later I received a fatter letter than usual from her. She'd enclosed two cuttings from her local newspaper. Each was headed rather grandly: *Reflections of an Airman* and each contained the bulk of a letter from me to her which she'd edited by removing personal information and had then sent to the paper. She'd opened an account in my name with the two cheques of fifteen shillings which the articles had earned me.

The editor, it seemed, hoped that *Reflections of an Airman* might become an occasional series.

It did and when I was back in England there were other series, for other papers. With stops and starts, this writing slowly became a career. Much later, in America, I got wind of Scott Fitzgerald, read *This Side of Paradise* and thought "I could do this" but of course I never could and I needed stunt and circus flying for many years in order to maintain an income until script writing came along and I moved eagerly for several years into one of those writer's rooms at MGM. The next war ended my screen writing and in 1946, thank God, I invented the pen name Rex Le Quesne, and the dozen or more thrillers I wrote about my dashing Welsh-New Zealander hero Zin Zan Owen gave me a secure income and the pension that has allowed me to grow into the decrepit wreck now writing this.

All that was years ahead though as I stepped off the

gangplank at Dover in late May 1919. I was longing to see Jessica, whose letters in reply to my regular ones had been intermittent, but I knew I had to see Constance. She was in the country though, so I prowled the empty house my parents had left me and mourned them as I hadn't had the health or time to do before. I remembered too as I sat in the silent living room, finally removed from the squadron and daily busy comradeship, the dead men I'd flown with. They were stuck then in my mind as they still are today in their energetic young bodies, with their unlined youthful faces.

I travelled west and took a room at The Love Arms. I'd never booked a room anywhere before but as I confidently negotiated this business, I realised how much I'd grown up in my eighteen months in the RAF. The landlord put me on the trail of what I wanted.

The cottage I rented sat just back from the village and I had it for six months at two shillings a week. It had been empty for some time. There were brambles and nettles in the garden that needed cutting back and piles of rubbish in the downstairs rooms that needed burning.

Two days later, with the morning sun pouring through the windows that I'd cleaned, and reflecting off the oak table that I'd found upstairs, polished and promoted to the kitchen, I felt I'd established a root somewhere that was my own. I hoped it would be a place where I could learn about the country. In my naivety I then imagined the country to be calm and peaceful; a place where I could write more *Reflections*, perhaps compile a book. Above all, the cottage felt like a secure base from which to deal with the two women only a mile or so away across the fields.

Constance was put out when I turned up. I hadn't written. I'd done what? When I could stay at the Hall? She looked a little askance at the tweed jacket and corduroys I now affected. "You look like a gamekeeper," she declared, though everyone was still ignorant then of Lady Chatterley.

Sir Richard was gruffly welcoming. We stood on the terrace in the sunshine.

"You must make the most of everything, my boy," he said. "You have to do the living for all those others, too."

Billy's medal had a table of honour to itself in the drawing room. As I heard Sir Richard speak of the presentation, I imagined his wait in damask-lined ante-rooms with other next of kin and recipients. I saw him easing his game leg as he perched on the crimson pile of a gilt chair and I heard the Marine Band in the gallery play a selection from *The Arcadians*. Then, as his and Billy's names were called, I saw him limp forward, disdaining his stick, to stand to attention before his sovereign.

"He was most kind and generous in his comments," Sir Richard said. "He seemed to know all about Billy and the squadron. And Captain Mitchell was immediately before me at the investiture. He spoke very highly of you both."

Two VCs for one unit at the same investiture was

unique but even then, when hearing of the squadron, the events of six or seven months before seemed a lifetime away. I remembered the pile of paper and the pencil I had left on the polished kitchen table and my sudden longing was for them.

The medal had a solid feel and the points of the Cross dug into my fingertips. The ribbon was a wonderful wine red and the words "For Valour", I found deeply if ironically poignant.

"You must be very proud, sir," I said.

"Occasionally," he replied. "But this piece of metal isn't worth it. I sometimes think despite it all, I would prefer my boys to be cowards and alive."

Constance was nowhere to be found, so after tea I walked back across the fields and found her perched on the bench to one side of my kitchen window. Her eyes were closed and her face was raised to the late afternoon sun. A beribboned sun hat lay at her feet on the grass I'd hurriedly hacked down the day before. Bees buzzed among the yellow roses that grew up the wall and framed her head where she sat. She turned at my step.

"What a charming spot you've found, George. May I have some tea?"

The obligatory tour of new dwellings followed and I soon found myself upstairs with Constance in my arms. She was as eager and obliging as ever but as we sank onto the bed, I knew that this place of my own wouldn't be my own if we continued; that I couldn't look after Jessica if Constance was still a presence in my life.

"What's wrong?" she said.

After a silence, I told her.

There were tears; mine as well as hers. I remember a wretched hollow feeling of panic. I hadn't even seen Jessica yet. She'd hardly written. I didn't know if she would want me but for this mirage I was giving up a woman like Constance.

Constance was pale. She said she loved me. Was there nothing she could do? Might I change my mind? She wept. I was deeply shocked by the change in her.

"I knew I couldn't keep you," she cried.

I hugged her and wept too as it dawned upon me how she felt and how she must have dreamt and agonised over me. Me! My head swam with the immensity of the realisation that I could cause such feelings. I said I was sorry over and over again.

Finally she pulled away from me and blew her nose.

"Thank you for being honest," she said. "I've been very foolish. Goodbye, George," she said, just before her feet clattered down the wooden staircase.

After a few minutes, I rose from the bed I'd remained slumped on. The sky had clouded over. I looked through the bedroom window and watched Constance a quarter of a mile away scattering sheep as she strode bareheaded and shadow less towards the copse that led to the Hall. I never saw her again after she disappeared among the trees. Below me on the grass outside the kitchen lay her forgotten sun hat.

I roused myself to call on Jessica, my plan all along for when my place was straight. The break with

Constance had come sooner than I'd anticipated but had been easier for being unpremeditated. My feelings, I believe, were confused. I was mortified to have caused Constance pain but strangely elated that the pain was genuine. It amazed me that apparently I had it in me to produce such devotion, such anguish in a grown woman. At the same time, there was relief that she would no longer try to organise me and would pester no more friends for me. Bubbling under everything though were memories of things we'd done that we would do no more.

And Jessica was at a dance in town, her mother said. I mooched back to my cottage, very unsure that I'd been right to confess all so soon. I put on my old flying helmet and goggles and kicked into life the ex-army Douglas motorcycle I'd bought for the equivalent of three years' rent. I thought I might see Jessica or somehow feel her presence more if I was in the same town.

I rode along the seafront in the failing light, threw pebbles at the waves, then putt-putted down a side street by the Town Hall to a pub that looked inviting. While Jessica danced in the arms of other men, I played dominoes and darts. I heard tales that might be worth retelling, though, and tried to keep a head clear enough to motor home.

At closing time, I pushed my motorcycle away over the cobbles, thinking to spare the sleeping seaside town its explosions as it started. Suddenly, white light burst from the Town Hall and flowed into the street. Shining couples came through the door that had opened. I paused in shadow across the road and heard them giggle and chatter their way off. Then Jessica emerged. A man's arm was around her shoulder. They turned, walked through a pool of light and dissolved into darkness. I slumped against the saddle in despair.

She had someone else. That explained the absence of letters. She'd soon forgotten me. And as for Billy...

There was a scream. It came from Jessica's darkness. I ran into it as I heard her cry, "Get off!"

I saw a light shape in the entrance to an alley. It was a thigh above a stocking top and Jessica's pale dress was above that.

I shouted something and ran full tilt into the man who was pressing himself against Jessica. He staggered, fell back, tripped and sprawled. Jessica immediately straightened herself and stepped back into the street. The man was getting to his feet. I shouted some nonsense to make him keep his distance. He held back but had the grace to call, "Jess, I'm sorry. I didn't mean to."

She stalked off up the road to the safety of the street lamp to wait for me.

"When did you come, George? How long have you been down here?" she asked at once, her assault sloughed off in an instant.

"Are you staying at the Hall?" But I wanted information before I gave any.

"Oh, Peter," she said, "I've known him for years. He always tries to kiss me. He's drunk too much I think. They had a vicious punch tonight. I hope he'll be all right. He was supposed to drive me home."

189

Bemused by her matter of fact tone, I explained my presence, told her of the cottage, led her to the Douglas. In the darkness, she slid her hand behind my neck and pulled my face down to hers. After our kiss, she held my face in her hands and when she said "Do you love me, George?" I said "Yes," without a thought.

I gave her my jacket and took her home side-saddle on my pillion. With our combined weight the Douglas laboured. The yellow headlight beam ahead illuminated the road and played over hedges, ditches, roadside trees. I fancied it was lighting our way into the dark future. Jessica's arm was tight around my waist and the fingers of her other hand gripped my belt. She'd laid her head against my back and I felt rather than heard her singing. The odd light in a cottage window marked our chugging progress through the night. It was a ride that I remember clearly for I've rarely felt as happy as I did then. The girl I'd just told I loved was clutching my waist and she trusted me to get her home while she sang to herself. Later, in my bed, I had more time to ponder Jessica's behaviour of that evening and wonder about it, though the recurring memory of her body against mine and of her kiss soon dispelled my worries. She hadn't said she loved me but she'd asked me if I loved her and had sung all the way home when I said I did.

I woke to the sound of cups on saucers from the kitchen.

"I've come for breakfast," Jessica called as I came downstairs. "I love your cottage. I'm going to make you some curtains. Look!" She pulled some string from her breeches pocket. "They'll be one long piece of string wide and one short piece of string long." Then she said, "I think you've had a visitor."

The hat Constance had left behind in the garden hung on the back of a chair.

"I hope she's gone."

I told her nearly all about Constance.

"You're a silly boy to throw a lady up," she said, keeping her eyes on the teapot she was filling. So I took the kettle from her and told her why I had.

We married in September, though she didn't agree that morning. I had a week or two of persuading.

"I'm not nice," she'd say. "You don't know. I'm ugly. I lose my temper. Sometimes I just want to be on my own."

I had answers to these simple protests but she went on.

"There's something I'll have to tell you that will make you hate me."

I laughed but when she told me, I was shaken and I didn't laugh. I gazed into her eyes, observed the sorrow there.

"I understand. It doesn't matter to me," I said and told myself it really didn't.

I had no answer though to the objection she never raised. Sometimes I'd catch her gazing sightless into the distance and knew that there was Billy still between us.

"No," she said when at last I mentioned him again. "I know he's gone. I'm not longing for him, just remembering." Her voice grew gentler than it sometimes was.

"Do you have memories?"

I offered her one. How cheered I would feel in France as he threw open the hut door and called, "What ho, George!"

We were sitting cross-legged on the grass in my garden. Jessica made a daisy chain on the lap of her skirt as we exchanged thoughts of our loved one. We stared into each others' eyes, hers were a grey-green, and developed a naked intimacy we hadn't shared before. She gave me the daisy chain but I doubled it and placed it on her head as a circlet. She sat carefully upright, took my hand in hers and described Billy's hand to me. I didn't mind. It was my hand she was holding.

Once, a shape in the corner of my eye made me glance up but what I'd seen was the shadow of a rose the breeze had blown. Billy wasn't there but his presence seemed to be, bringing validation to our conversation, benediction to our intimacy. A day or two afterwards, Jessica agreed to marry me.

After that, it was 1919 and a wonderful year to anyone who'd thought they might never see it and knew those who hadn't.

Jessica was still doing a little nursing and on those days I put paper on my kitchen table to write, or lay in a field with Keats, watching many a sailing cloudlet's bright career. As I did, I couldn't but remember what they looked like from above and how it was to throttle back and land on one, a solid seeming mass that your machine sank into, unless the throttle was opened again; and how around the next one might be the Hun that would kill you. It was only a year since I'd spent dawn to dusk days on that airfield near Bristol in the sun with the constant breeze that burnished your face and chapped your lips. Then I was preparing to fly or talking and listening, kicking my heels against the side of the oil drum I sat on. Two thousand feet above, in the sun, Mitch would be chasing one of our twisting, turning squadron mates, as likely as not dead now, like so many of them, like Billy. Like my mother and father.

But not me I thought and gloried in the thought, staring at the scarlet poppy blowing nearby above my head, delighted that such beauty as the sky, the cloud, the poppy, was still mine to enjoy.

My aunt wrote, anxious at my engagement. She was happy for me of course but how long had I known Jessica? Was I certain? Marry in haste, repent at leisure was her message. I reassured her. Jessica and I were deeply in love.

And we were. We walked hidden paths and rode the Douglas to the sea, where we bathed. I met her friends at parties, and there seemed to be many parties that first summer of peace.

It gave me a warm feeling to be wanted, to have an identity apart from my own. I quickly became known as Jessica's intended. No mention was ever made, in my hearing at least, of Jessica's previous intended. Perhaps the people she knew felt more comfortable for Jessica and for themselves in my more equal status compared to Billy's. Perhaps it was just normal human tact and English reserve. I know my acceptance by her friends gave a balance to the choice I'd made of renting a cottage and living alone to write.

I was so happy that summer that my mind bubbled and I contrived to have something published somewhere nearly every week. I became a regular at the post office and chugged carefully back from town one day with an Imperial typewriter strapped on behind me. If Jessica hadn't said yes and if I hadn't inherited a new family and group of acquaintances, I might at only twenty have shrivelled on the limb I'd crawled out onto. As it was, since I could withdraw from it often enough to cover the necessary sheets of paper, I suppose I blossomed and flourished in my new found family and circle of friends.

Now, I think my urgent pressure on Jessica to agree to marry me was partly a result of my sudden family void, a desire to find new people who might bother about me, to whom I might be important. Then, of course, no such thought occurred to me. When her hair was up and the curve of her neck and shoulder were exposed when we bathed at the beach or when her hand pressed the back of my head as we kissed or as I felt the sweep of her hip when my arm was round her, I knew it was desire that made me want her, not the promise of regular family lunches.

But it was good to have a family again. Jessica's father started calling me 'my boy'. He wore tweeds and a cap even in summer. His name was Gerald. I called him Mr Roberts. When he took me out after rabbits one evening, I imagined looking down on myself as I tramped the dusty path at his side with his second shot gun under my arm. I found the image difficult to credit even as I conjured it up. I found myself answering questions about family, education, the war; a future son-in-law quite reasonably being interviewed. Mr Roberts came from the area and still bore its accent despite education. He found my ignorance of the countryside alternately appalling and amusing.

"You'll soon learn," he'd say and since I'd learnt to fly an aeroplane, he was confident I would.

We climbed a gate into a meadow. The sun had fallen behind the hedge and we walked towards the sunshine that still lay on the far half of the field. Suddenly, he stopped, placed a hand on my arm and pointed. Twenty yards away, half a dozen rabbits, ears twitching around and up and down were eating in the sun. He motioned me to shoot.

I stared aghast at the defenceless creatures. But I'd come out to do it. It was dinner. I'd have to. As I raised the gun and cocked it, they set off in all directions. The one I'd selected scampered left. An instinct developed in the air made me automatically choose the right amount of deflection. I swung the gun ahead of it and fired.

The rabbit somersaulted head over heels, tumbled again and lay still. Mr Roberts was ecstatic. "You've never done this before?" he said. Perhaps I'd be all right after all, he probably thought. The rabbit's head was pulp, its body now just meat. We came across no more and we went home.

Lying in bed that night, I shot the rabbit again and again. I decided it was perfectly all right to eat meat and not want to kill for it. I decided I'd buy my meat at butchers' shops for I'd personally ended enough lives. Each time I saw the rabbit somersault, of course, I saw Billy fall. Each time I saw Gerald Roberts lift the rabbit to his bag and saw the head flop, the legs dangle, I felt Billy's icy hand that I had gripped farewell in the hangar they took him to and saw it fall helpless, lifeless, to his chest again when I released it, lifting it and letting it fall time and again, convincing myself that there really was no life there.

That vital, lovely man with his god's face a mashed gory mess from collision with the windscreen before he fell had become an undignified lump of meat no less than the rabbit had. I didn't trust myself to sleep that night until the room began to lighten.

My best man was Zin Zan and apart from my aunt, my only guest. He took three days off from barnstorming and we rode the Douglas back from town where we'd hired out suits.

Jessica liked him at once. We took out horses but he and Jessica outdistanced me immediately, racing off together along a moorland track, yelping and yelling as those Indians later would in his Western films. He was a wonderful horseman but Jessica was every bit as good. "She's a topper," he told me. "Lucky old George," he said, as if he couldn't believe my luck.

It was a classic wedding. The sun came out. Zin

Zan and I stood around nervously in our morning suits. I watched Jessica glide down the aisle on her father's arm, smiling only at me.

Jessica's mother cried. My aunt cried on my dead mother's behalf and when we were photographed outside the Norman church door, Zin Zan's smile shone out from the picture. All cameras loved him. We had cold ham and dancing and Zin Zan shone again. We had a dinner service from Sir Richard and Lady Love, though of course it was inappropriate for them to attend the wedding of their agent's daughter. The same went for Constance, though she sent a decanter. We left by sleeper for the Highlands, the trip a present from Jessica's parents. There were masses of midges, which were a trial, but then we stayed in a great deal. We were very happy and were still happy when we returned home.

Eight

I thought I'd all but told my story and had my ending ready but Pippa rang four days ago and invited me to visit. David came to drive me to her. After years in London, Pippa has moved to a small modern house in the village near the Hall that she grew up in, where I first met her when I visited with Billy in the summer of 1918.

David's kind laughter at my tales of Hollywood filled the car as we drove down the motorway at speeds not far off those we used to fly at. From time to time I'd see his head move almost imperceptibly as his eyes flicked constantly to mirrors, checking cars behind and to the side, much as Billy would have flicked his eyes around to check for Huns in French skies three generations earlier. Then suddenly I woke with the westerly sun full in my face. I looked round and was startled for a moment to see Billy smiling at me. David's look will sometimes take me unawares, like a slipped knife that cuts and shocks, for his nose, his smiling eyes, his hair, his laugh are all uncannily like Billy's.

Pippa was on her front path when we arrived. She is slim and white-haired and beautiful, with a stick for her bad hip. Her mother is in her but not as Billy is in David. She is outrageously amusing as I knew from our conversations on the phone and we chatted to each other like naughty children or long lost cousins till it was time for dinner at The Love Arms, where I'd stayed so many years before.

If you could somehow spirit all the vehicles away, the village would look much as it did when I came home from war. It threw me momentarily as I emerged from David's car that evening. It was the next morning though, as we made our way slowly around in the sun, that that year or so I'd lived there crowded back on me.

We came upon the cottage I'd rented back then for two shillings a week. It's pink and thatched and chocolate boxy now where once it had seemed rugged and sturdy but I saw it was essentially unchanged. I dare say even the yellow rose at the side may be the same one Jessica so loved when we were happy just after our wedding. I have a memory of that time, of just one moment really, which came to me again as I stared at the window the sun shone down on.

It's morning in our cottage kitchen and a still warm September sun falls through the window onto the flagstones. I sit in shirtsleeves at the table, from which I observe Jessica. We haven't long come from bed. Wearing just a cotton shift to her knees, a button at the top revealingly undone, she stands by the sink, checking the state of the garden through the window. Her hair is down and still tousled from sleep and with both hands she holds a teacup to her lips. Then as I raise my cup to drink, with fingers that still bear the scent of her sex, she turns and sees me watching her and smiles a gentle smile of recent love. It moves me still, that memory of happiness. To think it fled so rapidly.

Leaving the cottage and my memories, we drove to the Hall.

"How can you bear it?" I asked Pippa as we parked by the entrance. The gates had long ago gone for Spitfires. We peered down the drive.

"Fiddle-faddle, George," she said. "I'm glad that people use it." A stream of children ran from a side entrance towards the three minibuses drawn up outside the door that Billy slammed the night he argued with his father over Jessica; the night the fox killed the peacock; the night that Constance made a man of me, as they used to say.

Young faces stared as the minibuses passed us by and Pippa's former home, now a Field Study Centre, lay open to us if we cared to motor down. We looked at one another and Pippa asked David to drive on. He was taking her to see a friend who was unwell. I asked to be left to my memories on a bench by the churchyard. Cars drove past whose occupants would have labelled me the oldest inhabitant, an old buffer in the sun. David would return to heave open the great oak door of the church, which he and Pippa agreed would be too much for me. I was keen to see inside again although I knew what I would find there.

An era ended when Billy died, as it did for many families like the Loves all over England. There was no one to inherit the title and it lapsed. I'd known then that the estate would pass to Pippa, whose husband would have a different name. The family tombs in the church and churchyard, which ran in a continuous line from Elizabeth's day, would have no successors. As I sat on my bench in the sun, I feared I would see what I have often seen in country churches. Dragged in by weary parents, children with no knowledge of religion to make them reverential in the echoing stillness of the nave would skip unheeding past the polished brass plaques, like the one Sir Richard unveiled on the anniversary of Billy's death. Jessica and I attended the ceremony.

Capt. Richard Love MC
Somerset Yeomanry
1892 – 1916 Killed in Action
2nd Lt. William Love VC RAF
1899 – 1918 Killed in Action
Dulce et Decorum est Pro Patria Mori

Afterwards, unwilling to go home, Jessica and I walked through fields of stubble, separately silent with our own thoughts, until she stumbled badly in her heeled shoes and fell against me. I took her arm.

"I think I'm going mad," she said. "When the Vicar was talking about Billy, I wanted to sing. Something jolly, like 'Knocked 'em in the Old Kent Road', like we did when we went to the sea on your leave. And then the plaque! I was stifling giggles when Sir Richard unveiled it. That absurd little velvet curtain and the way it caught the first time and he had to try it again. I thought the whole thing would collapse. How Billy would have laughed!"

"But not then," I said, "he wouldn't have laughed then. It was too solemn a moment. A dead hero. He would have been moved."

We turned down a lane sunken between fields, with beech saplings shooting up between the pollarded oaks that rose from the banks.

"And is that him then, now?" Jessica said, "A few words in brass on a church wall?"

It's more than a million others are, was my unspoken thought.

I tapped my head. "He's still here and the Loves have him in their minds too and all those others in the church. It was half the estate, wasn't it? How many people would get that turn out?"

Jessica's laugh grated.

"They had to go, didn't they, with Sir Richard unveiling a plaque to his sons? They're all dependent on him."

I thought she was unjust.

"Many people were in tears, Jessica. He was well-loved. You know that better than anybody."

The brim of her black hat hid her face from me.

"By me you mean. Oh yes. I loved him. I loved him so much that I wouldn't do the one thing he wanted me to because otherwise he wouldn't marry me, when in fact he wrote to me practically every day and was at my house pretty well all the time he was home. I let my mother put that suspicion in my mind, and I left it there, mistrusting him. That's how I loved him."

"I'm sure he respected you all the more because of it."

She jerked away from my arm and swung round to face me.

"Oh," she said, "Do you think he'd have respected me then, when I went off into fields and shadows with those others, telling myself it was him I was making happy, granting his wish since he might be killed soon, letting them do what they wanted because I hadn't let him?"

Jessica had told me what she'd done after Billy's death, after I'd gone back to France; of the several men she'd gone with, soldiers due back at the Front, recovered from wounds. That was the secret that she'd promised would make me hate her. She was trying to destroy my resolve to marry her, despoiling herself in my eyes. She'd shocked me deeply. I hated to think of it; her back pressed to the grass in the dark, her fingers clutching khaki, the lunging weight on top of her; her despair; her self-deception; her loss of self-esteem.

"You weren't yourself," I said, "after your loss. You were disturbed."

"Disturbed? That's like mad, isn't it? I told you I was mad. Well," she pushed her face into mine, her hat brim threatening to hit my nose, a manic look in her eyes, a leer on her face, "what about it, dearie, would you like a nice time? It's not a dark alley like I'm used to but it'll do." She rubbed a hand over my groin and thigh, then pulled at my fly buttons as she clamped her mouth to mine and slid her tongue inside and around.

I was disgusted for a moment but almost as instantly aroused. My head filled with those visions of copulation that she'd tormented me with, which I might now swamp with my own brutal act of domination. We fell into each other's arms against the sloping bank. My weight forced itself between her legs. My fingers tore at her clothing. Excitement carried me away until I suddenly tasted salt. I paused to breathe and realised that she was lying very still, that her eyes were closed and that tears were forming pools on her eyelids. A wave of shame engulfed me. My lust subsided instantly. Was this how she'd been with those men she plagued me with, unmoving and weeping tears of silent self-reproach? I pulled her up, gave her a handkerchief and clutched her to me in case she fell. With Jessica sobbing from time to time, we stumbled home. Of course soon after that, since I was a budding writer, I put the whole episode in my journal where it's waited a lifetime for me to rediscover it.

I'd had no image before we married of the life that we would lead, except that I took for granted that I'd write, one day might have a study where I could turn out thick Hardy-esque novels while Jessica kept house. Meanwhile I'd read, prepare and Jessica would…? Well, in fact, she continued with some nursing and she rode in fiercely dangerous point to points.

Strangely for one who'd braved wood and canvas aeroplanes, my heart would be in my mouth. The danger seemed so unnecessary. There'd be no court martial for anyone who declined the risks she took but still she did it. I watched until I couldn't bear to, until one day, almost in front of me, she fell and Satan rolled on her and she lay so still for a moment that I thought she'd died. Satan stood nuzzling her, reins trailing. Before I could reach her, she knelt, pulled herself up on Satan's neck, remounted and was off again. We had our first words.

"What's life for if not to enjoy it!" she shouted. "You can't do much in the grave," and she stalked into the garden to prune roses violently. I stomped off for a walk and returned to find the kitchen table laid for dinner with a napkin over each of our plates. Together in stern silence we removed the napkins. My plate bore yellow rose petals, hers the thorns.

"My punishment," she said, rippling with laughter. That was characteristic of her swiftly changing nature. She was wilful and submissive, loyal but treacherous; a wonderful cook, who could burn a boiled egg; a wanton at night or in the afternoon, who might without warning seem to shudder at my touch. I could never tell which Jessica would appear. In my mind was a comparison with Constance, who was always calm, always equable. Jessica I'm sure compared me unfavourably with the boisterous, exciting and, we'd say now, charismatic Billy. Yet, though we each found the other wanting, I was captivated by the turn of her head, by the thinness of her wrists and, incomprehensibly, Jessica yearned for a baby from me.

I was horrified. Despite war service I felt little more

than a child myself and I was conscious of my lack of money. Though I had the house in London and a hundred in the bank that my parents had left me, I had no profession and the half-guineas and fifteen bobs my articles brought in might stop overnight if fashions changed. Six months rent on a cottage was as far ahead as I could see.

Constance had made me a disciple of Mrs Stopes and I was glad to follow her teachings to the letter, the French letter in fact, though Jessica threatened sabotage with a needle. I pleaded our poverty and the novel I wanted to write, when I might earn nothing for six months. It would be a tale of passion and the air. Two cousins: one German, one English, love the same girl. Torn apart by the war, they meet in the skies over Flanders. It was a plot I've since come across several times in print but then it was new and all my own and I could have been the first with it. Jessica claimed I wouldn't have a baby because I didn't love her. I replied it was *because* I loved her. And so on.

We rowed. Little things I did would make her angry, but a few minutes later her tone would be normal. Junket or apple charlotte? That was the kind of thing. I knew it mattered whether you had tracer every third round in your Lewis gun. If you didn't, you couldn't check your aim, but it really didn't matter whether our dessert was junket or apple charlotte. I loved them both and I had no opinion. Her irritation bemused me. My reaction to her behaviour was silent study; listening and watching. This had become automatic to me in new situations in the air force. It had been taken, I believe, for intelligence. Jessica took the same reaction, my lack of reaction, my failure to decide or get angry in return, as galling indifference, as lack of love.

Looking back, I can see how insufferable I was, how infuriating I must have seemed. But then I remind myself that I was only twenty. Back then I began to wonder exactly who I'd married, how I would come to terms with this person I realised I didn't really know at all. Of course we were entirely different, she and I, but since opposites attract, in life as well as in magnetism, we could perhaps have been all right.

Winter came. We lit lamps in the evening, wore all our clothes and barricaded ourselves into our cottage against the cold. Jessica sewed thick winter curtains. We washed each other's backs in the tin bath in front of the kitchen stove. We eased our chilblains with slices of potato and huddled together in bed.

People have had worse relationships and survived but with her changes of mood, which left me still smarting when she'd grown sweet again, I felt under attack, harried, as no air force superior had ever made me feel. We went to her parents for Christmas, a brief holiday in a warm house, with daily hot baths. Suddenly, the year after the end of the war was over. It was going to be 1920.

One evening I went upstairs after a night cap with her father and found her staring from the bedroom window at the frosted moonlit garden. Tears were streaming down her face. She was speechless and inconsolable and wept helplessly in my arms. I wept too. I longed to be what I couldn't be to her, what only Billy could have been, and when I reached that state, memories came flooding in of my parents and Billy and everyone I'd known who was dead. We were a fine pair and perhaps each needed a carer of our own but we only had each other and we weren't enough.

I found myself resenting Billy's place in her mind. If she could only think of me instead of him, things would be all right. To Jessica though, I'm sure, Billy was her perfect dead hero lover but she didn't have the luxury of public widowhood so she had to harbour and cherish his memory privately.

"You mustn't think of Billy with regret," I said one day when her humour was good and I thought it safe to speak. "You must let him go, and live your life as it is."

"I do not think of Billy," she said and, proving the reverse, left at once, heading across the fields for her parent's house, where Satan was stabled.

Those were the thoughts in my mind on that bench in the sun outside the churchyard when suddenly a voice interrupted them. Looking up, I saw a girl of ten or eleven, in jeans and a white tee-shirt. She'd asked if I was OK. I said I was and then with the direct coolness of pre-pubescence, she rapidly found out about me. She smiled a lot and I liked her immensely. Her name was Penny Hayter, a surname I remembered from Billy's day.

"I can open the church door you know, if you don't want to wait. You've been here a long time. I saw you."

I couldn't resist such a kind invitation and with much creaking of outer and inner doors, Penny ushered me solicitously through the porch into the cool dusty gloom of the transept.

"I'm glad someone's come to see Billy," she said. "We polished him last week so he's got a good shine on him. My mum's on the church rota. He's my favourite Love, though they go right back. My granddad used to work for them. Billy was very nice he says they told him. Was he?"

So, before she had to go, we sat in a pew beneath the shiny plaque and I told my young companion stories of the glorious Billy; how we'd met, what fun he'd been, the courage of his death. But after she was gone, in the still silence of the church, I found myself remembering again the sad days of my marriage. How I'd ached to be all things to Jessica! How I'd longed to change those sighs to laughter; her wistful distant gazes into smiles! How I'd anguished under my dilemma! For Billy had left me with a duty that ran against the truth I'd come to be certain of about his death.

The day that Billy died, when I packed his things up, I found that he'd left letters for Jessica and for his parents and also one for me. I've kept mine all these years and no-one else has ever read it. It was dated three days before he died and I still can't read it unmoved.

Dear George,
If you read this, I'll be dead. Please do all the usual things for me. Please send the other letters on and tell

the folks and Jessica what happened but spare the gory details. Instant death and all that please. Pa will read between the lines and you can tell him more in private if he asks.

I must apologise for all my funk and all the listening you've had to do. You've kept me to the mark through all this, for which many thanks. If I haven't disgraced myself by the end, please keep it under your hat.

Goodbye old chum and God Bless,
Yours affectionately,
Billy
PS. Please be a pal to Jessica, she may need one.

In the year and a half that had passed, and which had led to my uneasily married state, I'd had a lot of time to ponder Billy's death. One thought kept returning to my mind, a comment the balloon commander made, "He flew so directly, it was as if he didn't know the Hun was there." Then, too, I remembered the day before, the day that Pinner talked to us and took Billy under his wing after Billy had dived away and left the flight. When we'd all landed and the major stalked over to Billy's machine, his fury was horrifying. The major stopped and glared up to where Billy and the gunnery sergeant were standing on the wing examining Billy's Vickers gun.

"Damn it all, man!" I'd heard the major shout in the silence after the last of our motors stopped. "What do you mean by leaving a formation like that? You could have got us all killed!"

I'd just climbed down and I saw Billy's face turn ashen at the tone the major was using to him. The gunnery sergeant slid from the wing and stood to attention. Pilots hurrying together to discuss the flight stopped in their tracks, looking awkward. I took a pace or two then also stopped.

"Is there something wrong with Mr Love's gun, sergeant?" the major barked.

"Doesn't appear to be, sir."

"I managed to clear it in the air, major," Billy said.

"It often happens, sir," the gunnery sergeant said.

"I want a full technical report, sergeant. And you in my office now."

Billy followed him.

As they came past me, I heard the major speak to Billy in a hiss that the others heard as well.

"If you ever do that again, I'll shoot you down myself. Do you think you're the only one who's scared? I won't have any fucking skulkers in my squadron."

People gave each other embarrassed looks and, knowing of the friendship between Billy and me, one or two would not meet my eyes. I felt the taint that they were casting on him in their minds fall upon me, too.

Of course his last flight, our balloon protection patrol, was always in my mind as well. I turned it over constantly. There was the agonising Archie fire and the collision of poor Cameron and Kennington. Then the Fokkers dived on us and I caught sight of Billy turning away, leaving us to dive as if for home. The Fokkers were all engaged now and as I watched Billy in the far distance, beyond him, against the dark earth, I caught the glint of the sun on a brightly coloured wing and I instinctively kicked on the rudder bar and swung the control column left. The SE heeled over, its nose went down and I exchanged sky for earth in my vision as I chased after Billy.

A Hun had chosen the low route and his friends attacking us were merely the diversion. The balloon was now descending rapidly though it was still dangerously high. I was too far away to catch the Hun before he reached the balloon but I knew he might have friends behind him that I could deal with.

If I could paint, I could paint that picture still but what I painted would be streaks and flashes. Everything was in motion. Roads, splintered trees, smashed buildings disappeared faster and faster below my wings as my dive took me lower. In front, between my wing struts, Billy was tearing ahead. The Hun, with black crosses outlined in white now visible on its camouflage, was racing for the balloon and both grew in size as I drew closer. My engine was snarling as I reached a hundred and sixty miles an hour, heading for the Hun, who was hoping to reach the balloon before anyone caught him. Billy was above him and diving, hoping to cut the Hun off first, I thought.

The balloon commander on the ground later reported that he heard no gunfire. But if the Vickers had jammed and Billy had shot off the Lewis drum at long range hoping to put the Hun off, there would have been nothing to hear. It needed two hands and an undisturbed few moments to change the Lewis drum. It would have been impossible in a high-speed dive like Billy's.

Billy flew so directly and unflinchingly at the Hun, the balloon commander went on, that it was as if he didn't know the Hun was there. That thought suddenly leapt into my mind too during my diving pursuit and I uselessly yelled, "Look out!" over the engine's roar as Billy and the Fokker converged on that seemingly pre-ordained spot two hundred yards from the balloon, five hundred feet in the air. As I descended to Billy's height though, I saw he was a fraction higher than the Fokker. He meant to swipe the German's top plane with his wheels! Both might come off but Billy minus wheels would fare better than the Fokker with no upper wing.

In the final moment before the collision though, the German's training must have made him glance round and behind. He started a turn towards Billy. The Fokker rose a little, banked right and received the SE amidships.

Propeller and engine would have torn the German pilot apart. The two machines stopped dead for an instant but momentum swung the SE's fuselage over the top of the wreckage and catapulted Billy from the cockpit. Then Billy's goggles caught the sun and flashed his goodbye to me. I can still see him turning in the air, accelerating towards that terminal velocity we'd not known how to calculate, which mercifully his limp body showed he knew nothing of.

By those last sad days of my marriage, I'd re-lived that patrol a thousand times in my mind and after months of introspection I was finally certain how he'd died. When I added everything together: his behaviour of the day before, the failure to attempt to fire his guns, the headlong dash towards the enemy, and the balloon commander's statement, I was sure that Billy had been deserting us when he coincided in the air with that German and destroyed them both. A million to one chance or one in two according to my strange logic when talking with Billy on that airfield near Bristol: hit or miss. And he'd hit. He'd been trying to save his own skin by leaving his comrades in the lurch but it didn't matter to me I decided.

I hadn't really minded at the time it happened, but now in 1920, as a survivor with the war long over, I minded even less. I remembered Billy's kindness, his infectious good humour, the mischievous glint in his eye, his piratical gold-toothed grin and his haloed young god look at our first meeting. As well as all that, I remembered the day to day pressure of the work we'd been doing, a pressure that no one was ever born to bear. That was the strain that had bagged his eyes, made the side of his mouth twitch and led him to bite his fingernails to the quick. It had also caused an eruption of eczema on his arms and back that needed regular applications of cream to make the irritation bearable.

It was my hands that had rubbed the cream into his back for him and it was a service I'd carried out willingly. Now as I write this, I might even call it an act of love but searching my mind I recall no physical excitement. Perhaps it was there but buried deep by our instincts to survive in the daily horror we found ourselves experiencing. If excitement had been there though, I've often thought it might have surfaced to allow us in our fear to find comfort where we could on those sleepless nights we passed while exchanging terrors in the dark. Rubbing cream onto a bare back could easily have provoked further physical intimacies. It never did but I'm now convinced that physical attraction was a great part of the love I had for Billy. Added to his charm and kindness, he had a grace of movement and a face for which the only appropriate word is beautiful.

So, as I festered in my failing marriage, I accepted that he'd died while deserting me but understood that he'd suffered past all that he could endure. I, on the other hand, less sensitive than him perhaps and given one respite at a key time by my crash and another by my parents' deaths and my going down with flu, had never quite reached that breaking point. Even without the final request in his letter to me I would have known that out of love for him I must keep the secret of his cowardice just as I must care for Jessica. The dilemma of my youth, that I remembered so clearly in the church as I waited for David, was to be a pal to Jessica as I had pledged myself to be, while persuading her to love me, though her love was still all for her dead hero lover, whom I'd convinced myself was no hero at all.

Meanwhile, Satan was always Jessica's comfort and it was to him in his field that she went after the Hunt Ball. We'd argued again earlier in the day about a baby and she'd told me again that I didn't love her. She had a full card at the Ball and danced and danced, occasionally with me. At midnight I went outside to cool off and found her pressed against a wall, energetically kissing her most recent partner. He left in some embarrassment. The moon was shining on my face.

"Don't look at me like that, George," she said, and ran off.

I found her dress on the landing at home, where she'd pulled it off. Her breeches and boots had gone, so I knew where she was. I hesitated, but then, gazing down at the strewn dress, I saw again the man's hand on the silk covering my wife's breast.

I went to the field. It was empty. I sat on one of the large stones near the gate and smoked a cigarette. I stared across the moonlit grass and remembered standing there going on for two years before as she showed off her bareback riding tricks. Billy had been beside me then and I knew she still saw him when she looked at me. Well, I wasn't glad he was dead, but dead he was and the living were left and she was my wife and should start acting like it. Of course I know now that when you have to demand your wife should act like a wife, it's all up. But I was twenty then and it hurt.

I think I understand her behaviour a little better now. She was in love with the memory of Billy and the river of life was sweeping her away. I was the driftwood she clung to till she could reach land. Babies? Other men? From midstream, you can't judge solidity, you grab anything, reach for a trailing liana and hope it's a lifeline. Poor Jessica! We were both eaten up with our own concerns. I should never have persuaded her to marry me and she should have had the strength to turn me down.

In the field that night, I heard hooves that grew louder. I stood up. Jessica's white shirt was luminous in the moonlight, the grass was silver and Satan's dark coat had a weird unearthly sheen. They thundered towards me and Jessica pulled him up short as she'd done that previous time and slid effortlessly from his bare back to land a step from where I'd been standing. I'd already jumped away towards the gate in sudden panic – had she not seen me in the dark?

She laughed. "Poor old George! Always jumping out of the way. Always scared of something."

"Come home, Jess. I want to talk to you," I said.

"I don't want to talk to you," she said. "You spy on me."

"I'm glad I did," I said. "How far would you have gone?"

She laughed again.

I knew what was wrong with her.

"You must forget Billy," I pleaded. "All you've got is me."

"But you're not Billy," she wailed and despite my own pain I felt the deepest wave of sympathy for her. If she'd only stopped speaking then!

And she might have done but something disturbed Satan. He snorted, pawed the ground and moved threateningly towards me. I backed away of course.

"Look at you," she laughed, "he won't hurt. You're

frightened of everything. You won't have a baby. The horse scares you. How did you manage in the war? Did Billy have to nursemaid you?"

I suppose it was the sneering injustice that did it. I knew it was just a remark in a quarrel. She just meant that my approach to life was cautious where Billy's had been buccaneering. But I knew that it was Billy who'd flown for home when I'd turned with the flight to face the diving Huns.

"Billy was worth ten of you," she added. "He was frightened of nothing."

I should have walked away. I had no standing in Jessica's eyes. She preferred anyone's attentions to mine. It was all over. That mouth sneering at me had often moaned in my ear but the fingers gripping Satan's mane had only a very short time ago pulled another man's face down towards hers.

I knew I'd promised myself to keep Billy's secret and I knew I'd promised to be a pal to Jessica but I couldn't help myself.

"Actually you're wrong," I said. "The truth is Billy flew away from a fight and collided with that German by accident."

She was silent.

"He'd done it before. The major was going to shoot him down if he did it again but he hit this German and was suddenly a hero."

"You're lying," she said. "It's what you did, isn't it? You ran away and you're trying to say he did. He was trying to save your skin when he died, wasn't he?"

Then, God help me, I told her all about Billy's last

flight: the collision between Cameron and Kennington, the attack by the Fokker biplanes, his fatal and treacherous turn for home, how the balloon officer said "It was as if he didn't know the Hun was there."

Jessica's face set hard as she listened.

"You can say anything you like," she said, "and he's not here to defend himself."

"It's all true," I said. "I knew him."

That was the final stroke, my claiming knowledge that was hers alone.

"You never knew him." She let go of Satan's mane and came at me. "I knew him and he was better than you in every way."

She hit me with both fists on my chest, on my neck, again and again. She had the rings she'd put on for the Ball on the fingers of both hands. Her punches hurt. I know I only pushed her off, because I felt her breast squash beneath my hand. I suppose I pushed her too roughly. I was angry, too. Suddenly she was off balance. As she stepped back, she must have caught a heel on one of the stones and immediately caught the other as she moved it back to recover herself. She gasped and fell backwards away from my reaching hand. Unable to save herself, she took the full weight of her impelled body on the back of her head as it met one of the large rocks by the gate. I can still hear the awful finality of the slight grunt she gave before she ceased moving.

I bent over her, called to her, touched her cheek, but her head wobbled obscenely as if disconnected. Satan came and nuzzled her side and I pushed his face away. He snorted and returned. There was no pulse at her wrist that I could find and none at her neck. Had I got the right place? I felt for her heart and found nothing. I tried her wrist again. Nothing.

I felt a terrible aloneness in that field. "I've killed her," I remember thinking and that thought ballooned inside me until there was room for no others. I turned and climbed the gate and fled, leaving Satan nudging Jessica's side to wake her. After stumbling for a hundred yards or so down the dark path, I came to my senses. I was deserting her when perhaps I could still do something to save her.

I went back. Satan was still there standing watch. I checked Jessica's pulse again. What to do? I couldn't carry her. It was too far and in the dark the path was too treacherous. I laid my jacket over her and pulled off my shirt. I tucked it uselessly around her head. I couldn't make her more comfortable. Leaving Satan to guard her, I turned and strode off towards the village, fearing to run because a broken ankle wouldn't help her.

Eventually Gerald opened the door in response to my frenzied knocking and shouting. He took no notice of my bare chest but went straight to the hall telephone. As he waited for the doctor to answer, Jessica's mother came to the top of the stairs. Her hair was down from sleep and a white hand moved to her mouth as the realisation of what had happened came upon her.

"We had words," I told Gerald as we made for the field. "When I got home I realised where she'd gone. I found her there." I said no more. My implication was that Satan had thrown her. The doctor made a quick examination. "I don't know," he said. We lifted her onto the stretcher he'd brought. I took one end and Gerald the other. I led the way, leaving him to gaze down at his daughter's pale face. Down a path under trees we went, then through the sleeping village with moonlight turning windows silver. I was sure Jessica was dead and all the time I imagined her spirit watching me, accusing me. Only the memory of what I had told her about Billy's collision with the Fokker managed to replace that thought.

The doctor left us a bottle of whisky. I had several glasses. Then he was shaking me awake. I was flat out on a bench in his hall. "My boy," he said, "I'm sorry."

I walked out. Gerald was nowhere to be seen. Consoling his wife I imagined. It was just light. The one or two people I passed received no return greeting. At the cottage, I exchanged a sweater for the old jacket I'd taken from Gerald's coat rack and sat down. But Jessica was everywhere in the cottage and I couldn't stay there. Without knowing why, I found myself on the path to the field. I went through the gate and there a few yards away was the rock that had smashed her head. Her blood had dried on it.

Then behind me was the Vicar.

"The doctor told me. I saw you pass. I didn't want you to be alone."

Somewhere a shot rang out.

"Gerald said he couldn't bear to look at the beast," the Vicar explained.

I felt suddenly sick. The Vicar turned tactfully away

as I doubled over by the hedge. I noticed the cigarette end I'd tossed away the night before tucked conveniently out of sight alongside a stone. I hadn't mentioned waiting here for Jessica. I picked it up and slipped it into my pocket. I must have looked appropriately pale and dishevelled, for the Vicar was kindness and understanding itself. We'd had words I explained, young lovers. I'd drunk too much while waiting last night.

My memory had reached that point when the church door creaked and David came in full of apologies. A great-grandson, he'd been forced to chat with his great-grandmother's friends. He helped me up and out to the warmth of the sun. In the churchyard where he led me, the sun shone full on Jessica's grave in the plot that the Love's had given her father to lay her in. The grave was mown and weeded. The stone bore eight decades of lichen and weathering with nothing to show that she was the victim of another's hand, certainly not "loving daughter" or "beloved wife of", for there'd been no reason to tell the truth.

Everything was conveniently arranged. I persuaded myself it would serve no purpose to put myself forward for investigation. Jessica was dead. I couldn't bring her back. Satan was dead, I couldn't bring him back. Guilt pulsed through me in waves but how would a confession help? The Vicar would pray for us all he said.

It was terrible to see her parents. And I know the same was said of me because I overheard a snatch of conversation in the village shop. They put it down to grief and it was but I felt dreadful all day long and every day because I couldn't sleep at night either. I was prey to the most hellish dreams and I know it was guilt for though I told myself it was a dreadful accident, I was responsible. I'd promised myself to Billy and to Jessica and I betrayed them both when silence would have kept his secret, as well as her illusions and her life.

I gave up the cottage lease and rode my bike to London where I sold it. My aunt was distraught for me and I found I had to comfort her. Then a letter reached me and I bought a steerage berth for New York. Zin Zan was in a flying circus that needed pilots who could stunt to thrill the crowds. From there I went to Hollywood, to Canada, round half the world, then after forty years came back to England.

What of it all you may say?

There was a war and a terrible accident. A best friend married a best friend's girl but it was all a long, long time ago and besides, everyone but me is dead. Well, the past may be another country as they say but the mind lives there always, wherever it is that the body may travel. The plain fact is that Jessica was my one true love; my life's love. If Billy had lived, I would have been godfather to their children, visited at times, caught the curve of her neck in my eye, carried her gurgling laugh away with me. I would have loved her in silence. Billy died though and a tragedy followed.

I soon lost fear that my part in Jessica's death would be discovered but the shame and guilt my double betrayal caused has festered unspoken all my life. Till the day she died, Ruth, the woman I married in Hollywood, could never understand my occasional week long despairs and silences. Though she put it down to my war, it was conscience caused them all but I could never tell her.

So, at the sight of Jessica's grave, which David had led me to, those ancient doubts, which had slid into my mind almost at the instant of her death, came tumbling back. When Jessica was my living torment, I was certain that Billy had deserted us, was fleeing from the Hun attack. With Jessica dead that certainty had disappeared. How could I have been so sure? Billy had done it once he'd as good as confessed to me but had he done it again? Would he have done it again with the major's threat looming, with the importance of the patrol, with the squadron watching him?

Might it not have been that, while turning towards the attacking Fokkers, he'd glanced around as wary pilots should and spotted a glint of sun on the wing of the Hun who was making for the balloon? Had I not done that myself thirty seconds later? With no time to signal or warn the rest of us, what could he have done but swing his nose to the point of danger, "the only one of his flight" as the citation said "to see the lone intruder"? He would have known that only he could save the balloon, so he fired off the drum of ammunition on his Lewis gun to warn the Hun, to make him turn and thus buy time. He knew his Vickers gun had jammed and knew he would have to ram the German. Could he not have been the selfless hero everyone had thought? Could I not have been wrong when I so bitterly disillusioned Jessica?

I was gazing down at Jessica's grave, which I hadn't seen since her funeral, when David interrupted my thoughts. He pointed to the corner where the church walls met and said very quietly, "And don't forget that Billy is over here."

I took two steps past the corner. That was all that was necessary to reach the weathered stone engraved with RAF wings. I found myself in a daze. "What ho, George," I could almost hear Billy say. After a moment my eyes were so full that I could barely see. I hadn't known they'd lain so close for seventy years. I hadn't known that Billy's father had brought him back from France and buried him in another family plot. It was something I hadn't expected and hadn't prepared for and it moved me so much that, standing there, I could merely dab at the tears that streamed down my cheeks.

Their heads were a mere yard apart at the corner of the church. The same sun shone on both, the same rain fell on both and though their brutal deaths had parted them, at rest they were united.

Now, as I look out at the garden from my desk, I see the lime tree that was full when I began this tale is bare of leaves. Instead, they coat the lawn, as dense as gravestones in those cemeteries in France. I've written my story and leave it for David and for any others he may later choose to read it but my conscience is unrelieved. Although Jessica and Billy lie together in that quiet earth, as Cathy and Heathcliff do forever in that tale of passion that Jessica so loved, that does not assuage my guilt. I find no redemption in their presence there. I was called upon back then and failed. If what many believe is true and some future existence awaits me, perhaps I must soon face Billy and Jessica and bear their reproaches for my betrayal.

Or can I hope I will be spared that further suffering; that my conscience will just blow around the world to disappear eventually in fragments, as the ashes of those lime leaves will as they drift upwards in the smoke of the bonfire that will soon consume them?